CONTAINMENT

Jeff Atelier

To my wife, Carbon, whose own creativity showed me I had stories worth telling and lit the spark.
This is for you.

1

Day 1 - Morning

"You must be Rick." Alan's voice barely cuts through the mechanical thunder above them, the rotor wash whipping snow into frenzied spirals.

Rick squints against the assault, pulling his hood tighter. "That's right. And you're Alan?" His British accent carries through the cold, clipped and precise despite the circumstances.

Alan nods curtly, weathered face showing the strain of fighting the storm to get here. "Yeah, sorry to keep you waiting. This storm is one hell of a bastard, and we don't have much time." He gestures toward Rick's single bag with obvious concern. "Is that all you got?"

Rick shoulders the rucksack with a casual shrug, as if packing light for a six-month Antarctic assignment is perfectly normal. "Yes, this is everything." He pulls his jacket tighter as the wind whips up from the blizzard, ice crystals stinging his exposed skin.

Alan's expression grows more serious as he starts loading items into the helicopter, movements quick and efficient. "Alright, we better hurry before the storm picks up more. I'm told it's gonna be the storm of the century." He begins his preflight checks with practiced urgency, occasionally glancing at the darkening sky. "Get in the right seat while I finish my rounds." He doesn't look up from his instruments.

Rick circles around the front of the helicopter, ducking instinctively even though the rotors spin well above his head. The aircraft is older than he expected—military surplus, probably, with patches of primer showing through worn paint. Reliable enough to get him there, he hopes. If it gets him there, that's enough.

The passenger door resists when he pulls the handle, frozen mechanism protesting before giving way with a crack of breaking ice. The interior is cramped, utilitarian. No comfort features, just bare essentials. Rick tosses his rucksack into the space behind the seats, securing it with the cargo netting already mounted there. Professional setup. Everything tied down, nothing loose to shift during flight.

He hauls himself up into the co-pilot seat, the cold vinyl feeling like ice even through his thermal layers. The instrument panel spreads before him—gauges and switches he doesn't recognize, a world he doesn't belong to. Rick pulls the harness across his chest, the buckle clicking with satisfying finality. The five-point system is military grade, meant to keep pilots secured during combat maneuvers. Overkill for a transport run. Unless the weather really is that bad.

Through the cockpit window, Alan moves around the helicopter with methodical precision, checking connections, testing control surfaces, his lips moving in what might be a mental checklist. The man knows his machine. That's something, at least.

The pilot side door opens with a metallic groan. Alan settles himself down, immediately reaching for his headset. The familiar weight of it seems to calm him slightly as he gestures toward the spare set for Rick. His fingers dance across the control panel with muscle memory as the whirl of the blades begins to combat the wind from the oncoming storm. "All right, we're good to go."

Rick settles deeper into the unfamiliar seat, the helicopter's vibrations traveling through his body. "Bloody hell, it's cold." He rubs his hands together, breath visible even inside the cabin.

Alan glances over with mild curiosity, picking up on the accent despite the engine noise. "That accent, British?"

"Yes, that's right." Rick manages a slight smile despite the circumstances.

Alan's expression shifts to something like recognition, maybe even approval. "British? Served with some Brits back in the day. Solid soldiers. Professional." He adjusts their heading as they lift off, the landscape below becoming a blur of white.

Alan checks their instruments, then continues with what might be amusement in his voice. "You military?"

Rick's response is careful, measured. "Was. Long time ago now."

Alan's tone becomes more serious, professional, as he navigates through the increasingly turbulent air. "Right. Your military record is almost entirely redacted. This level of secrecy..." He trails off, letting the implication hang in the air between them.

After a moment's consideration, Alan presses further, his pilot's direct nature winning out over discretion. "Care to share what's hidden behind all this black ink?"

Rick's jaw tightens almost imperceptibly, gaze fixed on the white expanse below them. "No, not really. I was just following orders. That's all I can say." The words come out clipped, final, carrying the weight of things better left buried.

Alan nods slowly, recognizing the tone of someone who's carried secrets for too long. "Following orders. Well, that's exactly why you're here. It's not just about what you did." He banks the helicopter slightly, adjusting for wind shear.

His voice takes on an almost recruiting quality, as if he's trying to sell Rick on something he's not entirely sure about himself. "It's how you did it. Your ability to adhere to instructions without question. To perform tasks under the most extreme conditions without needing to know the why behind them. That's what makes you perfect for this role."

Rick turns to study Alan's profile, the tension around his eyes. "Perfect for the role? Or is it just because I can keep my mouth shut and do what I'm told?"

Alan's grip on the controls tightens slightly, knuckles whitening. "Both, actually. But it's more than just following orders this time. It's about ensuring safety, yours and others." He pauses, choosing his words carefully as if walking through a minefield.

"The tasks you'll be assigned are... Unconventional. Your experience, discipline, and ability to remain detached are invaluable." There's something in his voice that suggests he knows more than he's letting on, but is bound by his own set of orders.

Rick leans back in his seat, processing this information with the calm of someone who's heard similar speeches before. "Unconventional? Well, I've always been up for a challenge, and as long as the compensation reflects the secrecy and risks involved, I'm interested."

Alan's expression brightens slightly, as if relieved to move to more concrete territory. "The compensation is more than adequate. Trust me, you won't be disappointed. But money aside, what you'll find here, let's just say, it's a rare opportunity." His voice carries an odd mixture of excitement and apprehension.

He gestures toward the endless white landscape stretching below them. "A chance to be part of something few will ever know about, let alone experience. Threshold Station, the facility you'll be stationed at, is not your average research post."

Rick's curiosity is piqued, investigative instincts from his military days kicking in. "Threshold Station?" He pauses, considering the name. "Unusual designation."

Alan's response comes quickly, almost rehearsed. "It's an old name. Goes back to when the site was first discovered." He doesn't elaborate, instead focusing intently on his instruments.

Too quick. Rick catches the shift in Alan's body language, the way his shoulders tense. The man's deflecting.

Rick presses forward, voice carrying the authority of someone used to getting answers. "And what exactly will I be doing there?"

Alan's answer comes measured, as if he's reciting from a script he's memorized. "At Threshold Station, you'll be tasked with overseeing certain assets. It's a role that requires precision, diligence, and above all, mental strength."

The word 'assets' hangs in the air between them, loaded with implications. Rick's experience has taught him that when people avoid specifics, there's usually a good reason. And it's rarely good. "Assets? Are we talking about equipment here, or something else?"

Alan's discomfort is visible now, shoulders hunching slightly as he focuses on the controls. "Equipment, specimens, experiments. It varies. You'll be briefed fully upon arrival." The vagueness of his answer only raises more questions.

Rick leans forward slightly, investigative nature refusing to let this go. "Specimens? What kind of specimens are we talking about?"

Alan's response is sharp, almost defensive. "The kind that require constant monitoring and care. That's all you need to know for now." His tone makes it clear this line of questioning is closed.

But Rick presses on, voice taking on a harder edge. "Constant monitoring? Are we talking about biological materials? Animals?"

Alan's knuckles whiten on the controls as he grips them harder. "Rick, I'm not at liberty to discuss the specifics. You'll understand more once you're at the facility. Right now, I need you to trust that the briefing will cover everything you need to know."

Trust. The word hangs between them like a challenge. Rick has learned that trust in his line of work often means walking into situations where the full truth is deliberately kept from you until it's too late to back out.

"And if I don't like what I find when I get there?"

Alan turns to look at him directly for the first time since they took off, expression unreadable. "Then you stick it out for six months and collect your paycheck. That's the deal. No early departures, no matter what." The finality in his voice leaves no room for negotiation.

Six months. Rick turns the timeframe over in his mind. It's not that long, really. He's endured worse conditions for longer periods. But something about Alan's demeanor, the careful way he's choosing his words, suggests that these six months might test him in ways his previous assignments hadn't.

"What about the last bloke who had this job? Why did he leave?"

Alan's jaw tightens, and for a moment, Rick thinks he won't answer. Then, with obvious reluctance, he speaks. "The previous occupant... had difficulties adjusting. They completed their assignment, but..." He trails off, searching for the right words. "Let's just say the isolation can be challenging for some people."

Difficulties adjusting. Rick's trained ear catches the

euphemism immediately. In his experience, when people use phrases like that, they're usually understating something significant. "What kind of difficulties?"

"The kind that made them unfit to continue." Alan's tone is flat, making it clear he won't elaborate further. "Look, Rick, I get that you want answers. But some things you need to experience firsthand to understand. No amount of briefing will prepare you for what you're about to encounter."

Rick settles back in his seat, processing this information. He's dealt with classified operations before, assignments where need-to-know protocols kept even the operators in the dark about the bigger picture. But something about this is different, more personal somehow. The way Alan talks about the facility, about the previous occupant, carries an undercurrent of something that might be fear. Or maybe respect. Hard to tell which.

The landscape below them is nothing but white expanse interrupted occasionally by dark ridges of exposed rock. This is the most isolated place on Earth, thousands of miles from the nearest civilization, cut off from the outside world by weather and geography. Whatever happens at Threshold Station stays at Threshold Station. The thought is both liberating and terrifying.

"How often will I have contact with the outside world?"

"Limited." Alan's admission comes quick. "Communications are... unreliable out here. The magnetic fields around the facility interfere with most electronic equipment. You'll have a radio for emergencies, but routine contact will be minimal."

Magnetic fields. Rick files that detail away for later consideration. "And supplies?"

"Monthly drops, weather permitting. But the facility is fully stocked. You won't want for anything, physically speaking." The qualification at the end of that sentence doesn't escape Rick's notice.

They don't speak for a while, the helicopter fighting against wind currents that seem to strengthen the further south they travel. Rick watches the landscape below transform from merely desolate to absolutely alien. This is a place where humans were never meant to be, where every element of the environment is hostile to life.

"How much longer?"

Alan checks his instruments. "Twenty minutes, give or take. Weather's holding for now, but that could change quickly. If it does, we'll have to abort and try again another day."

The thought of being so close and having to turn back doesn't sit well with Rick. He's committed now, mentally prepared for whatever waits at Threshold Station. Having to delay that confrontation would only give his imagination more time to conjure worst-case scenarios.

"This storm that's coming." Rick nods toward the darkening horizon. "How bad are we talking?"

Alan's expression becomes grim. "Bad enough that I won't be able to get back in to check on you for at least a week, maybe longer. You'll be completely on your own until it passes." He pauses, then adds with what might be concern, "You sure you're ready for that level of isolation?"

Rick considers the question seriously. Isolation doesn't bother him the way it does most people. In fact, there's a part of him that welcomes it, a chance to escape the noise and expectations of the civilized world. His last assignment had left him with too many sleepless nights, too many faces he couldn't forget. Maybe six months in Antarctica is exactly what he needs.

"I'll manage."

Alan mutters it under his breath, but the headset picks it up clearly enough. "That's what they all say."

Before Rick can ask what he means, Alan points toward the windscreen. "There. That's Threshold Station."

Rick leans forward, straining to see through the snow and cloud cover. At first, nothing but more white expanse. Then, gradually, a shape emerges from the landscape, dark against the endless white.

"We can't land there." Alan begins their descent toward a flat area about half a mile from the facility. "The magnetic interference would tear the helicopter apart if we got too close. You'll have to walk the rest of the way."

Rick stares at the distant structure, trying to make out details through the deteriorating weather. From this distance, it looks like nothing more than a dark smudge against the snow, unremarkable and vaguely ominous.

"What is that place?"

Alan is silent for a long moment before responding. "It's... old. Really old. Older than any of us would have guessed when it was first discovered." He pauses, choosing his words carefully. "The company—whoever they are—they didn't build Threshold Station. They found it. They've been maintaining it, updating the systems, but the structure itself? That's been here a long time. Maybe centuries."

A chill runs through Rick that has nothing to do with the temperature. "Centuries?"

"The original structure, anyway. Victorian-era at least, maybe older. They've retrofitted it over the years—modern electronics, updated life support, new monitoring systems. But you can still see the age in the bones of the place." Alan's voice carries something like reverence. "Whatever you think it is, whatever you're imagining right now, you're wrong. Just... keep an open mind, Rick. And remember what I said about following instructions."

The helicopter touches down with a jolt, snow swirling up around them in a blinding cloud. Alan immediately begins his post-landing checks, hands moving with practiced efficiency across the controls.

"This is it." He kills the engine. "From here, you walk. Follow the flags if you can see them, but keep the facility in sight at all times. The weather can shift in seconds out here, and if you lose your bearings, you're dead."

Rick nods, pulling his hood up and securing it tightly. He grabs his rucksack from the back and double-checks that his torch is accessible. The idea of being lost in an Antarctic blizzard ranks high on his list of ways he doesn't want to die.

Alan's hand on his arm stops him before he can open the door. "Rick. One more thing." His voice is serious, almost pleading. "Whatever you see down there, whatever you experience... it's real. Don't try to rationalize it away or convince yourself you're imagining things. Just accept it, do your job, and get through the six months. Can you do that?"

It's real. The words send a chill through Rick that has nothing to do with the temperature outside. "What am I going to see, Alan?"

"I can't tell you that. But when you do see it, remember what I said. It's real. All of it." Alan releases his arm and sits back, expression troubled. "And Rick? Time... time works differently down there. Don't be surprised if the days start feeling strange. If you lose track of things. It happens to everyone."

The comment about time strikes Rick as odd, but before he can ask what Alan means, the pilot continues: "Now go, before the weather turns completely."

Rick opens the door and wind assaults him immediately, trying to peel the skin from his face. He steps down onto the snow, which crunches under his boots with a sound like breaking glass. The helicopter's rotors are already spinning up again as Alan prepares for immediate departure.

"Six months!" Alan shouts over the noise. "I'll be back for

you in six months! Good luck, Rick!"

The door closes, and moments later, the helicopter lifts off, banking away and disappearing into the grey-white soup of the sky. Rick watches it go until even the sound of the rotors fades to nothing, leaving him alone in a silence so complete it has physical weight.

He turns toward Threshold Station, barely visible through the swirling snow. Half a mile. It doesn't sound like much, but out here, in these conditions, it might as well be ten miles. Rick adjusts his rucksack, checks his compass one more time, and starts walking.

The wind is savage, coming at him from multiple directions at once, or so it seems. Snow finds every gap in his clothing, working its way inside despite his careful preparations. Within minutes, Rick's face is numb, exposed skin burning with cold. He keeps his head down, watching his feet more than the landscape ahead, trusting his sense of direction to keep him moving toward the facility.

This is why they pay so well. Rick had known the assignment would involve harsh conditions, but this... this is beyond anything he'd experienced before. Every breath is like inhaling razor blades, the cold so intense it hurts. His lungs ache with each inhalation, and he has to consciously remind himself to keep breathing steadily despite the pain.

Time becomes meaningless. Rick has no idea if he's been walking for ten minutes or thirty. The landscape offers no reference points, nothing to measure progress against. Just endless white in every direction, with the dark shape of Threshold Station growing larger ahead of him with painful slowness.

He tries to think about other things, to distract himself from the physical discomfort. Six months. What will he do with himself for six months in complete isolation? Alan had mentioned daily tasks, feeding schedules, monitoring protocols. That will provide structure at least, something to organize his days around. But the nights... the long, dark Antarctic nights that stretch for months...

Rick reaches into his jacket pocket and pulls out an energy bar, the wrapper crackling in the cold as he tears it open with his teeth. The bar is hard as a rock, nearly frozen solid, and he has to work it in his mouth for several seconds before he can bite off a piece. The calories are necessary, but eating while walking in these conditions is a challenge he hadn't anticipated.

As he chews the nearly flavorless bar, Rick thinks about the others who had made this same journey before him. Alan had been deliberately vague about previous occupants, but he'd mentioned them. How many people had walked this exact path? How many had stood where he's standing now, looking toward the same distant rise, carrying the same uncertainties and fears?

More troubling is the question of what happened to them afterward. Did they all complete their assignments successfully? Did they all walk back out of Threshold Station after their six-month tours? Alan's evasiveness about the previous occupant suggests that maybe not everyone's story had a simple ending.

The thought sends a chill through Rick that has nothing to do with the temperature. He's committed now, too far from the helicopter landing site to turn back, too close to his destination to quit. Whatever waits for him at Threshold Station, he's going to face it. But for the first time since accepting this assignment, he wonders if his confidence in his own psychological resilience might be misplaced.

The snow beneath his feet changes texture suddenly, becoming more compact, almost icy. Looking down, something has compressed the snow here—previous footsteps, perhaps, or the wind patterns around the structure.

The thought that others have made this exact journey before him is both comforting and unsettling. It means he's going the right way, but it also means that whatever lies ahead has been drawing people to it for some time.

The structure before him is nothing like what he'd imagined. Rick had pictured something more substantial—a proper research facility with multiple buildings, communications arrays, maybe even a landing pad. Instead, Threshold Station appears to be little more than a concrete bunker, surface weathered and stained by years of exposure to the harsh Antarctic elements. There are no windows, no external equipment visible, no signs of human habitation beyond the structure itself.

But there are details that immediately strike Rick as wrong. Despite the raging blizzard that had been battering him for the entire trek, the area around Threshold Station is remarkably clear of snow. Not just less snow—completely clear, as if there's some invisible barrier preventing the accumulation of ice and precipitation around the facility. The contrast is stark and unsettling, creating a perfect circle of bare, dark ground around the concrete structure.

As Rick descends toward the station, he becomes aware of something else: a sound that doesn't belong in this desolate environment.

Rick stops in his tracks, head tilting as an unnatural sound cuts through the howling wind. Wait, what the hell is that sound? Is that a generator, maybe? But it doesn't sound right. He strains to listen, but the noise comes from everywhere and nowhere at once.

It's not the steady mechanical hum of a generator or the rhythmic pulse of heating equipment. This sound is deeper, more organic somehow, like a massive heartbeat or the slow breathing of something enormous. The frequency vibrates through the ground beneath his feet, traveling up through his boots and into his bones.

The air around him begins to change as he approaches the snow-free perimeter. I can feel a weird vibration in the air. The sensation is similar to standing too close to massive speakers at a concert, where the bass notes don't just enter your ears but penetrate your entire body. A high-pitched ringing starts in his ears, persistent and unnatural.

Rick takes another step forward and immediately encounters resistance. It's not physical in the conventional sense—there's nothing visible blocking his path—but moving forward requires enormous effort. What the... why is it so hard to move? It's like something's pushing me back. What is this? Panic edges into his thoughts as he struggles against the unseen force.

Every step toward the facility now is like walking through increasingly thick liquid. The air itself has gained viscosity, pressing against him from all directions. His muscles strain against the invisible resistance, and he leans forward at an unnatural angle just to maintain his forward momentum.

His scientific mind tries to rationalize what he's experiencing, but the explanation sounds hollow even to himself. Is it some kind of magnetic field? This... this isn't normal.

The effects intensify as he pushes deeper into the anomalous zone. Rick's nose begins to run, but when he wipes it with his glove, dark streaks smear against the fabric. Blood. The realization strikes him with a spike of genuine fear—whatever force is emanating from Threshold Station is affecting him on a cellular level.

What the hell is happening? The metallic taste of blood fills his mouth as his nose continues to bleed. The vibrations in the air aren't just audible now; they're doing something to his body, affecting his circulation, his nervous system. The sensation reminds him of standing too close to powerful electromagnetic equipment, the kind of exposure that military personnel are warned about during training.

It's like being caught between two massive magnets with opposing polarities, the invisible forces pushing and pulling at him simultaneously. His body wants to retreat, every instinct screaming at him to turn around and run back the way he came. But he knows that's not an option—he's already committed too much to this assignment, traveled too far, and the Antarctic weather behind him is just as deadly as whatever lies ahead.

The struggle to reach the facility's entrance becomes a battle of will against physics. Rick has to rest every few steps, body shaking not just from cold but from the tremendous effort required to move through the field. Sweat pours down his face despite the freezing temperature, mixing with the blood from his nose and freezing on his skin.

When he finally reaches the concrete door of Threshold Station, Rick collapses against it, gasping for breath. The surface should be ice-cold against his face, but instead, it radiates a gentle warmth that seeps through his clothing and into his bones. The contrast between the bitter Antarctic cold he's just endured and this inexplicable warmth is disorienting.

Wrong. Everything about this is wrong. Concrete doesn't stay warm in negative forty degree weather. Nothing should be warm out here.

The door itself appears to be solid concrete with no visible handle or mechanism, but when Rick puts his shoulder against it and pushes, it gives way with surprising resistance. The interior beyond is nothing like what he expected from a research facility.

Instead of corridors or rooms, Rick stares at a single elevator shaft. But this isn't a modern elevator—it's an ancient-looking cage made of metal bars and grating, like something from an old mine. The kind of industrial lift that belonged in a different century, not a classified government facility.

Victorian. Alan said Victorian-era. Rick examines the rivets, the worn metal, the style of construction. This is original equipment, just maintained. How long has this been here?

Rick approaches cautiously and peers down into the shaft. The darkness below swallows his gaze completely, stretching down farther than his eyes can penetrate. He picks up a small chunk of concrete and drops it into the void, listening for the sound of it hitting bottom.

He waits. And waits. But no sound returns from the depths.

The entrance chamber is small, claustrophobic. Rick runs his hand along the wall, fingers tracing the junction where modern reinforcement meets original stonework. The contrast is jarring—smooth concrete poured over rough-hewn blocks that must predate the twentieth century by decades. Rivulets of condensation snake down the walls despite the cold outside, as if the structure itself is sweating.

In the corner, half-hidden behind a support beam, an electrical panel breaks the Victorian aesthetic. Modern. Out of place. Rick moves toward it.

The panel activates with a hollow click when he opens it, and illumination cascades down the shaft level by level, revealing just how impossibly deep the facility extends into the earth. Even with the lights, he can't see the bottom. Modern LED strips bolted to ancient stone walls. New wiring snaking alongside corroded Victorian pipework. They've updated it, but the bones are old. So old.

Rick hesitates at the threshold of the elevator cage. Every instinct tells him this is wrong, that descending into this unknown depth is madness. But he's come too far to turn back now, committed too much to this assignment to let fear stop him.

Taking a deep breath, Rick steps into the cage. The moment his weight settles onto the platform, ancient machinery grinds to life somewhere above. Without any input from him, the elevator begins its descent into the earth with a jerky, mechanical rhythm.

As the entrance chamber disappears above him and the cage carries him deeper into the facility, Rick grips the metal bars and tries to process what he's gotten himself into. The elevator operates with automatic precision, following some predetermined path into the depths. It was waiting for him. No call button, no controls, just waiting. Like it knew he was coming.

Like it's been waiting for him for a long time.

Right then. Don't start losing it before you even get there. But there's no denying it now. There's no turning back. This is it.

And somewhere in the back of his mind, a strange thought surfaces: This feels familiar. Like he's done this before.

But that's impossible.

Isn't it?

2

The slow grind of the elevator's gears echoes through the narrow shaft, a mechanical heartbeat counting down the distance between Rick and the surface world. Each metallic groan reminds him he's descending deeper into something unknown, each foot further from sunlight and fresh air and any hope of quick escape. The sound reverberates off the stone walls, creating a rhythm that makes it difficult to judge how much time passes.

How deep does this thing go? Rick cranes his neck upward, watches the entrance to Threshold Station shrink from bright opening to distant pinprick of light. The sensation disorients, like falling in reverse, and he grips the metal bars of the cage to steady himself against sudden vertigo. This isn't just a basement or sub-level—this is serious excavation, the kind of underground facility that takes years to construct and serious money to maintain.

When the elevator finally shudders to a halt, the silence that follows has physical weight. Rick's ears ring in the absence of mechanical noise, and he becomes aware of his own breathing, his heartbeat, the rustle of his clothing. His footsteps onto solid ground sound muffled, absorbed by the vast space around him.

The underground chamber stretches out before him, dimly

lit by fluorescent fixtures casting harsh shadows across aged stone walls. The air carries a cool, earthy smell—not unpleasant, but distinctly subterranean, like the inside of a cave or old basement. Something else underneath it, too. Faint chemical odor. Cleaning supplies, perhaps. Or preservatives. The space feels enormous in weak lighting, most of its boundaries lost in shadow.

Rick shoulders his bags and moves toward the only visible exit—a long hallway extending from the elevator chamber. The corridor narrows considerably from the vast space behind him, lined with dim lights providing just enough illumination to see a few feet forward. Here, his footsteps echo off the walls despite attempts to walk quietly, the sound traveling much farther than it should in the confined space. After several minutes, the hallway terminates at a simple wooden door—incongruously normal after all the industrial metal and stone.

The door opens into what is clearly his living quarters. The bedroom is spartanly furnished but functional: single bed with military-precise corners on the sheets, plain metal desk, tall locker that looks like military surplus, and a treadmill with free weights arranged in the corner. Everything has the impersonal cleanliness of a facility prepared for an occupant but with no personality of its own.

Bloody hell, this is it then. Six months in a hole. Rick sets his bags down, breathes deeply. Sharp smell of fresh paint and industrial-strength bleach. Recent enough the paint still has that slightly tacky texture when he runs his fingers along the wall. Someone really cleaned up in here.

Rick unpacks his kit methodically. Clothes in the locker, toiletries in the bathroom, personal items—what few he brought—on the desk. Standard routine. Keep it organized, keep it simple. When he reaches into his duffel for the last of his clothes, his hand brushes something on the shelf above the bed.

A leather journal. Weathered, spine cracked with age.

Rick pulls it down, turns it over. Date embossed on the cover: 1974.

Fifty-one years.

His chest tightens. How many people worked here before him? How many descended into this hole, unpacked their kit in this same room, found previous occupants' forgotten belongings? The journal is heavy in his hands, pages yellowed, filled with cramped handwriting. Someone's personal record.

Someone who left it behind.

Rick's about to open it when a voice crackles over the intercom, making him start.

"Rick? You there?" The voice is warm, professional, with a trace of concern. "This is Lily. I'm your primary contact for the duration of your assignment."

Rick sets the journal back on the shelf and moves to the intercom panel. Later. He'll read it later.

"Yes, I'm here."

"Welcome to Threshold Station. How was the descent?"

"Long."

Pause. What might be amusement in her voice. "That's one word for it. Listen, I know this is all a bit overwhelming, but I'm here to help you settle in. Why don't we start with a tour of your living quarters? I can walk you through everything remotely."

"All right."

"Excellent. First things first—you'll find a greenhouse through the doorway to your left. I know it seems unusual for an underground facility, but it's essential for long-term habitation. Fresh herbs, some vegetables, a few flowering plants. It makes a difference, trust me."

Rick moves through the doorway into the greenhouse. The

space startles him—lush green plants fill raised beds and hanging planters, creating a pocket of life in the underground complex. Herbs and flowering plants thrive under full-spectrum grow lights, leaves vibrant and healthy. Above it all, an automated sprinkler system mounts to the ceiling, network of pipes and nozzles designed for regular irrigation.

Someone actually thought this through. In a place this remote and isolated, fresh food would be impossible to obtain. The psychological benefits of caring for living things during a long assignment would be significant. Practical necessity and rare concession to human emotional needs.

At least I'll have something to do.

"It's impressive," Rick admits.

"I'm glad you think so. The previous occupant maintained it beautifully. You'll find detailed care instructions in the binder on the potting bench."

Previous occupant. The words sit heavy in Rick's mind.

Adjacent to the greenhouse, Rick discovers a compact medical bay. Shelves lined with bottles of supplements and basic medical supplies. Vitamin D dominates—multiple bottles, high-dosage capsules. Then calcium, B-complex, omega-3. His daily cocktail to compensate for a life without sunlight. In an environment this deep underground, maintaining basic health requires pharmaceutical intervention.

The bathroom is utilitarian but complete—shower, toilet, sink, all basic necessities for extended habitation. Everything clean and functional, but something sterile about it that makes Rick think of military facilities or institutions rather than homes.

The storage room reveals the reality of his situation more clearly than anything else. Rows and rows of canned goods line the shelves: chicken and rice, beef and carrots, corn, beans, fruit cocktail. Nutritionally complete but monotonously repetitive.

Great, no menu variety here.

But something catches his eye tucked away in the back corner. Box of coffee and cheap whiskey in a plastic bottle. Bottom-shelf liquor, the kind sold in corner stores to people who care more about alcohol content than taste. Not much, but it represents a small concession to the psychological challenges of isolation.

At least they're not complete bastards.

The kitchen is basic but adequately equipped with everything needed to prepare simple meals from stored provisions. A small refrigerator hums quietly in the corner, the countertops clean and ready for use. He's lived in worse conditions during military deployments.

But it's the communications room that really captures his attention. Banks of monitors line the walls, screens dark but ready. Thick cables snake between pieces of equipment that looks like it belongs in a different era—not quite modern, but sophisticated in its own way. The centerpiece is an intercom system that appears to be the primary means of contact with the outside world.

Bloody hell, this stuff looks ancient. Rick runs his hand along one of the terminals. The equipment has the worn patina of decades of use, buttons polished smooth by countless fingers.

How long has this place been operating?

Above the monitors, an electronic clock displays the time in large red numerals: 12:32 PM. Christ, it's already been three hours. The clock seems oddly prominent for a simple timepiece, positioned where it can't be missed, large enough to be read from anywhere in the room.

"The communications equipment is quite old, I know," Lily's voice comes through clearly now, no longer crackling. "But it's been maintained meticulously. Everything works.

And I'm always available if you need anything."

"Noted."

"You sound like a military man."

Rick pauses. "Was."

"Ah. That explains a lot. Don't worry—I won't pry. But it's good to know you're trained for structured environments. Makes the transition easier."

Something about the way she says it feels personal rather than procedural. Like she actually cares.

"The cell blocks," Rick prompts, redirecting.

"Right, of course. Why don't you head down the main corridor? I'll talk you through the layout."

————————————————

The corridor leading to the cell blocks is different from the rest of the facility. Older. The walls are rough-hewn stone rather than finished concrete, and the lighting dims considerably once Rick passes through a heavy metal door marked with a faded yellow warning sign. Temperature drops several degrees.

This is the original structure. Victorian-era mining facility, Lily said. Everything before this was modern retrofit, but down here—this is what Threshold Station was before it became whatever it is now.

"You'll notice the temperature change," Lily's voice echoes through the intercom speakers mounted along the corridor. "The original excavation runs deeper than the modern facilities. Try to keep that in mind if you start feeling disoriented."

"Understood."

The corridor opens into a wider chamber with three doors, each marked with a simple letter: A, B, C. The doors are heavy industrial steel with small observation windows, and each one has two separate entry points—an inner door Rick can control, and an outer door that appears automated.

"This is your primary work area," Lily explains. "Cells A, B, and C. Each one requires daily monitoring and maintenance. The procedures are straightforward, but they must be followed precisely. Safety protocols exist for a reason."

Rick approaches Cell A, peers through the observation window. The interior is dim, maybe three meters by three meters, empty except for what looks like a metal grate in the centre of the floor. Another door on the far wall—the outer door—is larger, more heavily reinforced.

"What's the outer door for?"

Brief pause. "The feeding protocol. We'll go over that in detail before your first assignment. For now, just familiarize yourself with the layout."

Feeding protocol. Rick's stomach tightens. He moves to Cell B, then C. Identical layouts, same two-door system, same metal grates in the floors.

"The grates," Rick starts.

"Drainage and disposal," Lily interrupts smoothly. "After each procedure, you'll use them to clear the cells. There's a hatch in the ceiling of each cell for access during cleanup. Everything's designed to minimize direct exposure."

Direct exposure to what?

Rick doesn't ask. Not yet. He's learned when to push and when to wait.

"The observation monitors in the communications room will give you full visibility of each cell," Lily continues. "You'll become very familiar with them. But for now, I think that's enough. You've had a long journey, and there's no point overwhelming you with too much information at once."

"When's my first shift?"

"Today, actually. Four o'clock. I know you just arrived, but there's no point delaying. Better to start right away, get the first one behind you."

Four o'clock. A few hours from now. Christ.

Day 1 - 3:30 PM

The alarm pulls Rick from equipment inspection in the communications room. Harsh electronic beep that makes his jaw clench. He's been waiting for this all afternoon, trying to prepare for whatever "feeding protocol" actually means, but the alarm still startles him.

"Right on time," Lily's voice comes through the intercom. "Ready?"

"As I'll ever be."

"Good attitude. First feeding is always the hardest. After that, it becomes routine."

Rick doubts that, but he doesn't argue.

"I'll walk you through step by step," Lily continues, her tone shifting to something more clinical. Professional. "First, check the monitors. Verify Cell A's inner door is secure."

Rick moves to the monitor bank, locates the camera feed for Cell A. Empty cell, both doors closed. The image is grainy, black and white, but clear enough.

"Inner door secured."

"Excellent. Now, at exactly four o'clock, the outer door will open automatically. It's controlled by a timer system—nothing you need to do. The procedure takes approximately fifteen minutes. During that time, you stay in the communications room. Do not approach the cell. Do not attempt to observe directly. Use the monitors only."

"What am I monitoring for?"

"Completion of the procedure. You'll know when it's finished."

That's not an answer, but Rick lets it pass.

"After the outer door closes, you'll wait thirty minutes before beginning cleanup. That's critical, Rick. Thirty full minutes. The cell needs time to stabilize."

"Stabilize from what?"

"You'll understand soon enough."

The clock reads 3:58 PM. Rick's pulse quickens despite attempts to stay calm. He keeps his eyes on the monitor showing Cell A.

"Two minutes," Lily says quietly.

Rick's hands grip the edge of the desk.

4:00 PM.

On the monitor, nothing happens. Rick leans forward, squints at the grainy image. Maybe the system malfunctioned. Maybe—

Then the outer door begins to move.

It opens slowly, mechanically, revealing darkness beyond. Not the darkness of an unlit room, but something deeper. Something that seems to absorb light rather than simply lack it.

And then—sound.

Even through the concrete walls, through the sealed communications room, Rick hears it. A wet, tearing noise. Shuffling. Something moving with purpose, with hunger. The microphones in Cell A pick up more—sounds that make Rick's hindbrain scream warnings his conscious mind can't quite process.

Whatever entered that cell is feeding.

Rick forces himself to keep watching the monitor. The darkness beyond the outer door shifts, pulses, but he can't make out any distinct shape. Movement without form. The sounds continue—ripping, crushing, something wet hitting the floor.

His hands are shaking.

"Steady," Lily's voice, soft but firm. "This is normal. It's supposed to sound like that."

"What is it?"

"Focus on the monitors, Rick. We'll discuss details later. For now, just observe and confirm the procedure completes correctly."

The sounds grow louder, more violent. Something slams against the wall inside Cell A—the impact visible on the monitor as the camera shakes. Rick's breathing comes faster, shallower. Every instinct screams at him to run, to get out, to put distance between himself and whatever is in that cell.

But he stays. Because he needs this job. Because he signed the contract. Because running would mean questions he's not prepared to answer.

The feeding continues for twelve minutes.

Twelve minutes that feel like hours.

Then, abruptly, silence.

The outer door begins to close. Slowly, mechanically, sealing whatever was beyond it back into darkness. The door shuts with a heavy clang that echoes through the facility.

Rick exhales. Didn't realize he'd been holding his breath.

"Well done," Lily says. "Your first procedure completed successfully. Now we wait thirty minutes before cleanup begins."

"What was I feeding?"

Pause. Longer this time.

"The facility's primary specimen," Lily answers carefully. "That's all you need to know for now. Focus on your responsibilities, not the bigger picture. Trust me, it's easier that way."

Primary specimen. The words sit wrong in Rick's mind, clinical and deliberately vague. But he's too shaken to push further.

"Thirty minutes," he repeats.

"Exactly. I'll check in when it's time."

Thirty minutes pass in a blur of attempted calm and failed distraction. Rick paces the communications room, tries to focus on equipment checks, anything to avoid thinking about what he just witnessed. The sounds replay in his mind on loop—wet tearing, heavy impacts, that awful shuffling movement.

This is the job. Monitor, report, survive, get paid. Don't think. Don't question.

"Rick?" Lily's voice breaks through his thoughts. "Time for cleanup. You'll find protective equipment in the storage locker outside Cell A."

Rick moves down the corridor on autopilot. The storage locker contains heavy rubber apron, thick gloves, respirator that looks like something from a chemical weapons facility. He suits up mechanically, hands still trembling slightly as he fastens the apron.

"Remember," Lily's voice echoes through the corridor, "you'll access the cell through the ceiling hatch. There's a ladder mounted to the wall. Do not open the inner door directly—the hatch is specifically designed for safe entry after procedures."

Rick climbs the ladder, positions himself above Cell A's ceiling hatch. The metal is warm under his hands. He turns the wheel lock, feels it release, and pulls the hatch open.

The smell hits him even through the respirator.

Blood. Fresh blood, with undertones of something else. Something organic and wrong.

Rick descends into the cell on the mounted ladder, keeps his eyes focused on the rungs until his feet hit the floor. Then he has no choice but to look.

The entire room is covered in blood. Fresh blood, glistening under the fluorescent lights. It coats the walls, pools on the floor, spatters the ceiling in patterns suggesting violence rather than accident. The metal grate in the centre is clogged with—

Don't look too close. Don't think about it.

Rick's military training surfaces, allows him to process the scene with professional detachment even as his mind reels. His eyes are drawn to the outer door—the larger one that opened automatically. Strange markings carved around its frame. Symbols he doesn't recognize but which seem ancient, deliberate.

Not random scratches. These were carved with intention, precision. Ritual or ceremonial purpose.

What were they keeping in here?

Rick forces himself to begin cleanup. The protocols are clear: hose down the walls first, then the floor, washing everything toward the central drain. Let the grate handle the bulk of it, then use the industrial chemicals for what remains. Simple. Mechanical. Don't think about what you're cleaning.

The blood is thick, viscous, still warm in places. Rick works methodically, spraying down one wall at a time. The water runs pink, then red, then darker as it mixes with what accumulated on the floor.

Is this human? Animal? Something else?

He can't tell. Too much blood to determine source. Could be pigs, cattle, something large. Remote location would make regular livestock deliveries impractical. Maybe that's what this is—some kind of feeding system for supplies. Clinical, efficient, processed underground where conditions stay controlled.

Rick wants to believe that. Needs to believe that.

The cleanup takes ninety minutes. By the end, the cell

looks almost normal again. Almost. Faint stains remain on the concrete, shadows of what happened here. Rick climbs back out through the ceiling hatch, seals it behind him.

His hands shake as he strips off the protective equipment.

"Cleanup complete," he reports over the intercom.

"Excellent work," Lily responds. "I know that was difficult. First time always is. Why don't you take the rest of the evening off? Get some rest, process things. Tomorrow will be easier."

Rick doubts that.

But he nods anyway, even though she can't see him. "Right. Thanks."

"Rick?" Her voice softens. "You did well today. Really well. Most people struggle a lot more with their first procedure."

The words should comfort him. Should make him feel competent, capable.

Instead, they just make him wonder how many people she's said that to before.

Day 2 - 8:00 AM

Rick wakes to the alarm on his watch after a night of fractured sleep. Dreams of blood and darkness, sounds that didn't quite make sense, shadows that moved wrong. He'd given up on the bed entirely, slept on the floor beside it. Felt safer somehow. More controlled.

Morning routine helps restore normalcy. Workout on the treadmill—pushing until his muscles burn and his mind empties. Shower. Bland chicken and rice breakfast. Vitamin cocktail. All mechanical, all routine.

But the quiet gets under his skin. The isolation feels heavier today, like the facility itself is pressing down on him. No windows, no natural light, no way to judge time except by the clock in the communications room. Just endless underground chambers and the memory of yesterday's feeding procedure.

Rick's checking equipment in the communications room when Lily's voice crackles through the intercom. Different from yesterday. Less formal, more... concerned?

"Morning, Rick. How are you feeling?"

"Fine."

"Didn't sleep well, did you?"

He pauses. How does she know that? Then he remembers —surveillance. Monitors. They probably track everything down here, including whether he actually uses the bed.

"First night's always rough," Lily continues before he can respond. "The isolation takes adjustment. Believe me, I understand."

"Do you?"

"More than you'd think." Something in her tone shifts. Personal rather than professional. "I've been managing Threshold Station for five years now. I know what it's like to be disconnected from the world. To feel like you're the only person who exists."

Five years. Rick tries to imagine it—five years of this facility, these procedures, the endless isolation. "That's a long time."

"It is. But it becomes routine eventually. And honestly? Having someone to talk to makes all the difference. That's why I try to check in regularly. Not just for procedures, but for... conversation. Human connection."

Rick doesn't respond immediately. Part of him appreciates the gesture, the acknowledgement that this isn't just a job but a psychological challenge. Another part—the part trained in interrogation, in recognizing manipulation—stays wary.

"I appreciate that," he says carefully.

"Good. Because I meant what I said yesterday—you

handled your first feeding procedure exceptionally well. Most people panic, refuse to continue, demand extraction. But you stayed calm, followed protocols, completed cleanup efficiently. That speaks to real professionalism."

The praise feels genuine, but Rick has learned not to trust his instincts about such things. Still, it's nice to hear. Validation after yesterday's horror.

"Military training helps."

"I imagine it does. May I ask what branch?"

"British Army. Deployed to Afghanistan twice."

"Ah. That explains the composure under pressure." Pause. "Must have been difficult. Coming back from that."

Rick's jaw tightens. She's probing now, gently but deliberately. Looking for information, building rapport. Standard intelligence technique—establish common ground, encourage the target to share personal details, create emotional connection.

He knows what she's doing.

But isolation makes it harder to resist. Harder to maintain professional distance when she's the only voice he hears, the only human contact in this underground tomb.

"It was," he admits. Keeps it vague. Doesn't elaborate.

"Well, if you ever want to talk about it—or anything else— I'm here. Not as your supervisor, but as someone who understands what isolation does to people. Sometimes it helps to have a listener."

"Noted."

Lily seems to sense his discomfort, shifts topics smoothly. "Today's procedure is Cell B at four o'clock. Same protocol as yesterday, but you'll find each cell has slightly different characteristics. Cell B tends to be... louder. Just so you're prepared."

Louder. Christ.

"Understood."

"I'll check in before the procedure. Until then, feel free to explore the facility, maintain the greenhouse, whatever helps you settle in. And Rick? Don't hesitate to use the intercom if you need anything. Even if it's just conversation."

The line clicks off before he can respond.

Rick sits in the silence that follows, processing the interaction. Lily's offer of support feels genuine. Her understanding of isolation, of what this place does to people, seems authentic. But he can't shake the training that taught him to question everything, to see manipulation even in kindness.

Maybe she really is just trying to help. Maybe that's all this is—one isolated person reaching out to another.

Or maybe she's building something. Creating dependency. Making herself indispensable.

Rick doesn't know which possibility worries him more.

Day 2 - 4:00 PM

The feeding procedure in Cell B is worse than Cell A.

Lily was right about it being louder. The sounds that come through the walls—through the monitors—are more distinct, more visceral. Rick can hear individual impacts, the wet crunch of something breaking, screaming that doesn't sound quite human but close enough to make his stomach turn.

He forces himself to stay in the communications room, keeps his eyes on the monitors even though he wants to look away. The darkness beyond the outer door pulses and writhes, and something inside that darkness moves with terrible purpose.

Fifteen minutes.

Fifteen minutes of sounds that will haunt his dreams.

When the outer door finally closes, Rick's hands are

clenched so tight his nails have drawn blood from his palms.

"Steady," Lily's voice comes through softly. "You're doing great. I know it's intense, but you're handling it perfectly."

Rick can't respond. Can't find words.

"Take a few minutes," Lily continues. "Breathe. Ground yourself. The cleanup can wait."

Ground yourself. Standard trauma response technique. Rick recognizes it, appreciates it, even as he resents needing it. He focuses on his breathing—four counts in, four counts hold, four counts out. Military training kicking in. Calm the nervous system, regain control.

After several minutes, his hands stop shaking.

"Ready?" Lily asks.

"Yes."

The cleanup is worse than Cell A. More blood, more viscous, and something else mixed in—fragments he doesn't want to identify. Rick works mechanically, hosing down walls, washing everything toward the central drain, not thinking about what he's clearing away.

When he finally climbs out through the ceiling hatch, his entire body aches with tension.

"Cleanup complete," he reports.

"Excellent work, Rick. You're adapting quickly—faster than most. That's impressive."

Rick strips off the protective equipment, hands still trembling slightly. "Doesn't feel impressive."

"Trust me, it is. Most people need weeks to reach your level of composure. You're handling this remarkably well."

The praise should feel good. Should provide some satisfaction. Instead, it just makes Rick wonder who she's comparing him to. How many people has she watched go through these procedures? How many adapted, and how many broke?

"Rick?" Lily's voice interrupts his thoughts. "I know today

was difficult. Why don't you take some time for yourself this evening? Make a proper meal, maybe have some of that whiskey you found. You've earned it."

She knows about the whiskey. Of course she does—surveillance everywhere, monitors tracking every room.

"Might do that."

"And Rick? I meant what I said earlier. If you need to talk, I'm here. About the procedures, about adjusting to isolation, about anything. Sometimes it helps just to have a conversation with someone who understands."

Rick considers this. Weighs the offer against his trained caution, against the isolation that's already starting to press heavier.

"Thanks," he says finally. "I'll keep that in mind."

Day 3 - 10:00 AM

Rick spends the morning in the greenhouse, finding unexpected peace in the routine of tending plants. Watering, pruning, checking for signs of disease or nutrient deficiency. The work is simple, mechanical, but it provides something the rest of the facility lacks—evidence of life, of growth, of something other than death and darkness.

He's inspecting the herb garden when Lily's voice comes through the intercom.

"Finding some zen in the greenery?"

Rick jumps slightly, hadn't expected her to check in so early. "Something like that."

"It helps, doesn't it? Having something to care for. Something that responds to attention and effort."

"It does."

"The previous occupant was quite dedicated to the garden. Spent hours in there each day. I think it kept him... stable. For a while, at least."

Rick's hands still on the basil plant he's been examining. "What happened to him?"

Long pause. Too long.

"He completed his contract successfully," Lily says finally. "Left on good terms. But toward the end, I could tell the isolation was getting to him. The garden helped, but eventually, even that wasn't enough."

"How long did he last?"

"Full six months. Like I said, completed his contract. But it changed him. This place changes everyone."

Rick wants to ask more—wants to know what "changed" means, wants to understand what happens to people after six months in this underground tomb. But something in Lily's tone suggests she won't elaborate.

"Fair enough."

"Rick, can I ask you something?" Her voice shifts again, becomes more personal. "Why did you take this assignment? The money's good, obviously, but most people don't accept positions like this without... reasons. Something driving them."

There it is. The question Rick knew was coming eventually. She's been building to this since yesterday, establishing rapport, creating space for personal disclosure.

He should deflect. Should maintain professional distance.

But the isolation makes honesty appealing. Makes the possibility of genuine human connection worth the risk.

"Needed to disappear for a while," Rick admits. "Needed distance from... complications."

"Complications."

"The kind that follow you if you stay in one place too long."

"Ah." Something knowing in her tone. "Legal trouble?"

"Not exactly. More... moral trouble. Did something I

shouldn't have. Can't undo it, can't fix it, can't face it. So I ran."

The words surprise him as they leave his mouth. He hasn't admitted that to anyone, hasn't even fully admitted it to himself. But isolation strips away pretense, makes confession easier than performance.

"We've all got things we're running from," Lily says softly. "That's why places like Threshold exist. They offer what the world can't—complete separation. Anonymity. Time to process without judgment or consequences."

"Is that why you've been here five years?"

Pause. Then a quiet laugh. "Touché. Yes, I suppose it is. I made mistakes too. Did things I couldn't take back. This job offered escape without having to face myself. And honestly? It's easier here. Simpler. No messy human relationships, no complicated emotions. Just procedures and protocols."

Rick's surprised by her candor. Surprised she's sharing this. Unless—

Unless it's calculated. Unless this is part of building trust, creating false intimacy. Make him feel like they're both damaged, both running, both understanding each other in ways no one else could.

But it works anyway. Because even if it's manipulation, even if she's playing him, the isolation makes him grateful for it.

"I understand that," Rick says.

"I thought you might. There's something about you, Rick. A kind of... recognition. Like you see the world the way I do. Most people I work with, they're either desperate or deluded. But you're different. You understand complexity. Moral ambiguity. The grey areas where most people can't survive."

The words should set off alarms. Should trigger every warning sign his training taught him to recognize. But instead, they just make him feel understood. Seen.

Christ, I'm already compromised.

"Thanks," Rick manages.

"I mean it. You're handling this exceptionally well, and I think that's because you're not fighting against the reality of this place. You're accepting it. That's rare."

Rick doesn't respond. Can't decide if he's being praised or assessed.

"Anyway," Lily continues, tone lightening, "I didn't mean to get philosophical on you. Just wanted to check in, make sure you're settling in all right. Today's procedure is Cell C at four o'clock. Same as the others, but Cell C tends to run longer. Sometimes up to twenty minutes."

Twenty minutes. Rick's stomach tightens.

"Understood."

"I'll check in before the procedure. And Rick? Thanks for being honest with me. It means a lot to know I'm not the only one down here carrying baggage."

The line clicks off.

Rick stands in the greenhouse, surrounded by thriving plants and gentle grow lights, and tries to untangle what just happened. Lily revealed personal information, created sense of shared experience, positioned herself as ally and confidante.

It's textbook manipulation.

But it doesn't feel like manipulation. It feels like genuine connection.

Rick's trained to spot the difference, trained to maintain objectivity. But isolation makes training less reliable. Makes loneliness more persuasive than caution.

He returns to the basil plant, tries to focus on something simple and mechanical. But his mind keeps circling back to Lily's words.

You're different. You understand. We're in this together.

Standard manipulation phrases. He knows they are.

But knowing doesn't make them less effective.

Day 3 - 4:00 PM

Cell C's feeding procedure lasts nineteen minutes.

Nineteen minutes of sounds that make Rick question his sanity, his choices, his entire understanding of what's possible. The darkness beyond the outer door seems more active this time, more aggressive. Something inside that darkness pounds against the cell walls with force that shakes the camera feed.

Rick grips the edge of the desk and forces himself to keep watching. Forces himself not to run, not to break, not to fail.

You're handling this exceptionally well. That's what Lily said. That's what he needs to be—exceptional. Capable. Someone who doesn't break under pressure.

When the outer door finally closes, Rick exhales shakily.

"Excellent," Lily's voice comes through. "See? Easier each time. Your body's adapting to the stress response."

Is it? Rick doesn't feel adapted. He feels like he's barely holding together, like one more procedure might shatter whatever composure he's maintained.

"Take your time before cleanup," Lily continues. "And Rick? I'm proud of how you're handling this. Really proud. You're proving everything I thought about you—you're stronger than you give yourself credit for."

The words land differently now, after this morning's conversation. Less like professional assessment, more like personal encouragement. Like she actually cares.

"Thanks."

"Why don't you come back to the comms room after cleanup? I'll be here. We can talk, help you decompress. This is the hardest adjustment period—once you get through the first week, everything becomes routine."

Rick hesitates. "All right."

The cleanup is as bad as the others. Blood and violence and fragments he refuses to identify. Rick works mechanically, doesn't think, doesn't process. Just hoses down walls and watches pink water swirl down drains.

When he finally returns to the communications room, stripped of protective equipment and exhausted, Lily's voice comes through immediately.

"Hey. You all right?"

Rick sits heavily in the desk chair. "Honestly? No. But I'll manage."

"I know it's overwhelming. But you're doing remarkably well, Rick. Better than anyone I've worked with recently."

"How many people have you worked with?"

Pause. "Enough to know exceptional adaptation when I see it."

That's not an answer. Rick wants to push, wants to demand numbers, specifics. How many people worked here before him? How many completed their contracts? How many broke?

But he's too tired to fight.

"Thanks," he says instead.

"Listen," Lily's voice softens. "I know this is difficult. I know you're questioning whether you can handle six months of this. But I want you to know something—you're not alone. I'm here, every day, every procedure. We're in this together."

We're in this together.

The phrase should trigger warning signs. Should remind Rick of manipulation techniques, of creating false intimacy. But instead, it just feels comforting.

"I appreciate that."

"Good. Because I mean it. You're different from the others, Rick. There's something about you that makes me think you can not just survive this, but actually understand it. The facility, the procedures, what we're doing here—it's not just work. It's important. And I think you see that."

Rick doesn't see that at all. Doesn't understand what this place is, what they're feeding, why any of this exists. But Lily's words make him feel special. Chosen. Like he's part of something significant rather than just a isolated worker in a hole.

"I want to understand," Rick admits.

"You will. In time. For now, focus on adapting. Getting through each day. Building routine. And remember—I'm here whenever you need to talk. About procedures, about isolation, about anything. You're not alone in this."

You're not alone.

The words wrap around Rick like warmth, like safety. Like Lily actually cares about him as more than just another contracted worker.

Maybe she does. Maybe this isolation affects her too, makes her reach out to the only other human voice in the darkness.

Or maybe that's exactly what she wants him to believe.

Rick's too tired to figure out which.

Day 4 - 7:00 AM

Rick wakes to familiar nightmares—Kandahar, the interrogation room, the moment everything went wrong. But now the nightmares blend with newer images: blood-soaked cells, darkness that moves, sounds that shouldn't exist. Past trauma and present horror mixing until he can't tell which memories are real.

He's given up on the bed entirely now. Sleeps on the floor, back against the wall, positioned where he can see the door.

Old habits returning, military instincts surfacing under stress.

Morning routine provides structure. Workout, shower, breakfast, vitamins. Mechanical motions that keep the mind from spiraling.

Lily checks in during his equipment inspection. "Morning. How are you doing?"

"Managing."

"Nightmares?"

Rick pauses. "How did you—"

"Your heart rate was elevated during sleep. Consistent with nightmare patterns. It's normal, Rick. This place affects everyone's sleep. But it gets better."

It's invasive—monitoring his heart rate, tracking his sleep patterns. But Rick finds he doesn't mind as much as he should. Finds it almost comforting that someone's paying attention, that Lily actually notices when he's struggling.

"Thanks for checking."

"Of course. That's what I'm here for." Pause. "You're not eating as much. I've noticed."

Rick glances at the monitor, reminded again that she sees everything. "Not particularly hungry."

"That's the stress. Try to maintain your nutrition anyway. Your body needs fuel, especially with the physical demands of cleanup."

"I'll manage."

Another pause, longer this time. "Rick, you're doing well. Better than well, actually. But don't push yourself too hard. It's okay to struggle with this. It's okay to need support."

The concern in her voice sounds genuine. Feels genuine.

"I'm fine," Rick says. Automatic response, military deflection.

"All right. But I'm here if that changes." She shifts gears. "Today's Cell A again. Should be routine by now."

Routine. Rick tries to imagine these procedures becoming

42

routine, becoming something he can witness without horror. Can't quite picture it.

"Understood."

"I'll check in before the procedure. Until then, try to rest. Get your mind off things. You're doing great, Rick. Really great."

The line clicks off.

Rick sits in silence. Four days, and Lily's voice has become the only human connection in the darkness.

He's not sure when he started depending on it.

Day 4 - 3:30 PM

The alarm sounds as usual, but something feels different today. Heavier. Like the facility itself is holding its breath.

Rick moves to the communications room, checks the monitors. Cell A looks normal—empty cell, both doors closed. Everything standard.

"Ready?" Lily's voice comes through.

"Yes."

"Good. Standard protocol. I'll be monitoring throughout."

The clock ticks toward 4:00 PM. Rick's pulse quickens despite attempts at calm. His hands grip the desk edge, knuckles white.

4:00 PM.

The outer door begins to open.

And then—

Christ.

The sounds are different this time. Louder, more violent, more visceral. Something slams against the cell walls with enough force to shake the camera. The darkness beyond the outer door doesn't just pulse—it writhes, churns, moves with terrible hunger.

And the screaming.

Rick's heard screaming before. Combat zones, interrogation rooms, places where people break. But this screaming doesn't sound human. Doesn't sound like anything from the natural world. It's frequency wrong, pitch distorted, like vocal cords attempting sounds they weren't designed to make.

"Steady," Lily's voice cuts through the horror. "This is normal. Stay focused."

Normal. Nothing about this is normal.

The feeding becomes more aggressive. Rick can hear ripping, tearing, something heavy hitting the floor repeatedly. The camera shakes so hard the image blurs. Whatever's in that cell is destroying it.

Fifteen minutes.

Fifteen minutes of violence that makes previous procedures seem gentle by comparison.

When the outer door finally closes, Rick's breathing comes in shallow gasps. His shirt is soaked with sweat, hands trembling so hard he has to clench them to maintain control.

"Rick?" Lily's voice, concerned now. "Talk to me. You all right?"

"What the bloody hell was that?"

"Just a more active feeding cycle. It happens sometimes. The specimen's behavior varies."

"That wasn't variation. That was—"

"Extreme, I know. But you're safe. The facility's secure. The procedures work."

Rick wants to argue, wants to demand answers. But his training kicks in—regain control, assess situation, respond tactically. Panic helps nothing.

"The cleanup," he manages.

"Wait forty-five minutes today. The cell needs extra time to stabilize."

Forty-five minutes. Rick nods, even though Lily can't see him.

"Rick, you did perfectly. Stayed at your post, maintained observation, didn't panic. That's exactly what we need. I'm proud of you."

The praise feels wrong now. Feels like consolation for witnessing something he shouldn't have.

But Rick accepts it anyway. Because what else is there?

Day 4 - 5:15 PM

Rick descends into Cell A through the ceiling hatch, prepared for the usual blood and violence.

He's not prepared for the carnage.

The entire cell looks like an abattoir. Blood coats every surface—walls, floor, ceiling—so thick in places it's still pooling. The stench cuts through the respirator, makes Rick's eyes water. But worse than the blood is the damage. Deep gouges in the concrete walls, chunks of stone torn away. The reinforced outer door is dented inward, metal warped by impacts that should be impossible.

Christ. What kind of strength does that?

Rick forces himself to begin cleanup, but his hands shake as he operates the hose. Water mixes with blood, runs in thick rivulets toward the central drain. Fragments wash toward the grate—he tries not to look at them, tries not to identify them.

But then he sees it.

In the corner of the cell, partially hidden under a pool of blood.

A human ear.

Rick's stomach drops. He moves closer, needs to confirm what he's seeing. Needs to be certain before his mind accepts the implications.

It's definitely human. Unmistakable shape, size, structure. Fresh enough that it's still pliable, still—

Rick turns away, breathes hard through the respirator. Human. That's human tissue. Which means the blood is human. Which means whatever's being fed to that specimen isn't livestock or animals or any other sanitized explanation.

They're feeding it people.

The realization hits like physical impact. Rick's knees weaken, and he has to grip the ladder to stay upright. They're feeding it people. Jesus Christ. All this time, all these procedures, he's been facilitating murder. Has been cleaning up after—

"Rick?" Lily's voice crackles through the intercom. "Status update?"

Rick can't respond. Can't find words.

"Rick, I need confirmation that cleanup is progressing."

"There's..." Rick's voice comes out strangled. "There's an ear. Human ear. In Cell A."

Silence.

Then: "Dispose of it through the hatch. Continue cleanup. File your report afterward."

"Lily, this is human. This is a person. What the hell are we —"

"Continue cleanup, Rick. We'll discuss this after you've finished."

The line clicks off.

Rick stands in the blood-soaked cell, staring at the human ear, and understands exactly what he's become. What this facility is. What he's been part of.

They're feeding people to something in the darkness.

And he's been helping them do it.

Day 4 - 7:00 PM

* * *

Rick strips off the protective equipment with shaking hands, doesn't care that he's getting blood on the floor. Doesn't care about protocols or procedures. His mind races with implications, with horror, with the growing realization that everything about this facility is wrong.

He storms to the communications room, slams his hand on the intercom. "Lily. Explain. Now."

Brief pause. Then her voice, measured and calm: "Rick, I understand you're upset. But you need to calm down and listen carefully."

"Calm down? You've been making me feed people to—to whatever the hell is in those cells. You've been making me clean up murder scenes. And you want me to calm down?"

"It's not murder, Rick. It's containment."

"Containment?"

"The specimen in those cells is dangerous. Extremely dangerous. It requires feeding to remain stable, to stay controlled. The individuals provided are already deceased—we're not killing anyone. We're managing something that, if left unchecked, would cause devastation beyond anything you can imagine."

Rick's mind spins, trying to process the explanation. "You're feeding corpses to a creature in the basement."

"Essentially, yes. Carefully sourced, properly documented. Everything we do here is necessary. Vital. And I know it's horrifying, I know it challenges everything you thought this job was. But Rick, you've been doing important work. Essential work."

"Essential work." Rick's voice breaks. "Christ, Lily. You should have told me. You should have—"

"If we'd told you, you never would have accepted the position. No one would. But now you understand the stakes. Now you see why this facility exists, why we maintain these procedures. The specimen must be contained. Must be fed. Must be managed. Or people die. Many, many people."

Rick wants to argue. Wants to reject the explanation. But part of him recognizes the logic, understands that something kept in cells this reinforced, fed this carefully, must be genuinely dangerous.

"Who were they?" Rick asks quietly. "The people being fed."

"Does it matter?"

"It bloody well matters to me."

Lily sighs. "Criminals. Individuals who were already facing execution in various jurisdictions. Their deaths were inevitable—we just... repurposed them. Gave their deaths meaning."

Rick's stomach turns. The rationalization is smooth, practiced. How many times has Lily given this explanation?

"And the previous occupants?" Rick presses. "The people who worked here before me? What happened to them?"

"Most completed their contracts successfully. Left with substantial compensation and NDAs that ensure they never discuss what they experienced here."

"Most."

"Rick—"

"What happened to the ones who didn't complete their contracts?"

Long pause.

"They broke," Lily admits finally. "Couldn't handle the psychological pressure. Some demanded extraction early, some had... episodes. But everyone who requested evacuation received it. No one was forced to stay."

Rick's mind races, trying to piece together the truth from Lily's careful words. The journal on his shelf—1974. Fifty-one years of operations. How many people worked here? How many adapted, how many broke, how many left changed?

"I need to think," Rick says.

"I understand. Take time. Process this. But Rick—please understand that what we're doing here is necessary. The specimen must be contained. And you've been doing that job perfectly. Exceptionally, even."

Rick doesn't respond. Can't respond.

"I'm here if you need to talk," Lily continues, voice softening. "I know this is overwhelming, I know it changes everything. But you're not alone in this. We're in this together."

We're in this together.

Rick ends the call without responding.

He sits in the communications room, surrounded by dark monitors and ancient equipment. The journal on his shelf flashes through his mind—1974, fifty-one years ago. He should read it. Should learn what the previous occupant experienced.

But not tonight. Tonight his brain is full. Tonight he needs to stop thinking.

Day 4 - 10:00 PM

Rick finds himself in the storage room, staring at the plastic bottle of cheap whiskey he'd discovered on Day 1. He'd planned to save it. Ration it carefully over six months. Be responsible.

Sod it.

He cracks the seal, takes a pull straight from the bottle. Burns going down, chemical aftertaste, but the warmth spreads through his chest. Takes the edge off the horror. He takes another drink.

They're feeding people to something in the darkness. Criminals, Lily said. Already dead. Repurposed.

Rick laughs. Actually laughs. The sound echoes wrong in the empty storage room. Repurposed. That's one word for it.

Another drink.

His feet carry him to the greenhouse without conscious decision. The grow lights are on their night cycle, dim and blue-tinged. The plants seem to glow in the artificial twilight. Living things. Green things. Normal things.

Rick sits on the potting bench, bottle in hand. The basil needs pruning. The tomatoes need staking. Simple problems. Fixable problems. Not like human ears in blood-soaked cells.

He drinks and prunes. Drinks and stakes. His movements grow looser, less precise. The whiskey helps. Helps him not think about the screaming sounds during the procedure. Helps him not see the ear when he closes his eyes.

The trowel slips from his hand, clatters to the floor. Rick bends to retrieve it, overbalances slightly, catches himself on the raised bed. Laugh again. Bloody brilliant, Rick. Can't even pick up a trowel without making a production of it.

He sets the trowel on the edge of the potting bench. Means to put it away properly but forgets. It leans against something —pipe? Support beam?—doesn't matter. He'll sort it tomorrow.

Rick takes another pull from the bottle. Maybe a quarter gone now. He should stop. Should drink water, take vitamins, sleep.

Should read that journal.

But his body is heavy, mind pleasantly fuzzy at the edges. The horror from earlier feels distant now. Manageable. Just a job. Just containment. Necessary work.

He can handle this. He's handled worse.

Right?

Rick makes his way back to his quarters, leaves the half-empty bottle on the desk. Collapses onto the floor beside the bed—still can't bring himself to sleep on the mattress. Floor feels safer. More controlled.

Sleep comes quickly. Deep and dreamless. The whiskey does its job.

Behind him in the greenhouse, the trowel leans precariously against the irrigation pipe. Over the next few hours, condensation from the watering cycle slowly weakens the seal where trowel meets valve connection. Not enough to cause immediate failure. Just enough to start a hairline crack that will grow, slowly, over the next day.

Days 5-7

The routine reasserts itself.

Rick wakes on Day 5 with a pounding headache and fuzzy memories of the greenhouse. He swears off the whiskey. At least for a while. The vitamin cocktail helps, and by mid-morning he's functional again.

The 4:00 PM procedure happens. Cell B. Same as before— sounds, darkness, cleanup. But this time Rick knows what he's cleaning. Knows what he's feeding. The knowledge sits heavy in his chest, but he completes the task. Files his report. Lily checks in, warm and concerned.

"You're doing well, Rick. I know yesterday was difficult, but you're adapting. That's exactly what we need."

Day 6 passes similarly. Workout, greenhouse maintenance, equipment checks. The 4:00 PM alarm. Cell C. The screaming from beyond the outer door doesn't sound quite so alien anymore. Still disturbing, but... expected. Part of the rhythm.

Rick tends the greenhouse that evening. The plants are thriving under his care. He's gotten good at pruning, watering, maintaining optimal growth. Something he can control. Something he can succeed at.

He notices moisture on the floor near the irrigation system

but dismisses it. Condensation, probably. This deep underground, everything's damp.

By Day 7, Rick realizes something unexpected: he's settling in.

The morning routine feels natural now. The isolation, while heavy, isn't unbearable. The procedures are horrifying, yes, but they're also structured. Predictable. He knows what to expect, how to respond, what's required.

Lily's evening check-ins have become comfortable. Familiar. She asks about his day, offers advice on the greenhouse, makes conversation that feels genuinely human. They talk about books, music, what life was like before this assignment. Nothing deep, nothing that requires him to be vulnerable. Just... company.

"One week complete," Lily says on Day 7 evening. "How are you feeling about everything?"

Rick considers the question. "Better than I expected, honestly. It's not easy, but it's manageable. The work is... well, it's necessary. You were right about that."

"I'm glad you see it that way. And Rick? You're doing exceptionally well. Better than most people at this stage. There's something about you—a resilience, I think. An ability to adapt and function despite difficult circumstances."

The praise lands differently now. After the horror of the ear, after the explanations, it feels earned rather than manipulative. Rick has proven himself. He hasn't broken. He hasn't demanded extraction.

"Thanks. That means something."

"Get some rest. Week two starts tomorrow. It'll be easier now that you understand what we're doing here."

The line clicks off.

Rick sits in his quarters, looking at the journal on his shelf. The 1974 one he found on Day 1. He's been meaning to read it, kept meaning to, but there's been no urgency. No pressing need to know what the previous occupant experienced.

Maybe he'll read it this weekend. Or next week. There's time. Six months of time.

He's got this handled.

The thought brings unexpected comfort. One week down, twenty-three to go. But if this week taught him anything, it's that he can adapt. Can survive. Can do the necessary work.

Rick lies down on the floor beside his bed—habit now, feels more secure than the mattress—and closes his eyes.

Tomorrow is Day 8. Week two begins. The routine continues.

In the greenhouse, water seeps slowly through the crack in the irrigation pipe. The pressure increases. The seal weakens.

But Rick doesn't know that yet.

For now, he sleeps. Dreamless and still.

Convinced he's finally getting the hang of this place.

3

Day 8 - Week 2 Begins

The alarm on Rick's watch pulls him from sleep at 6:00 AM. He sits up—on the bed this time, not the floor. Sometime during the second week, he'd started trusting the mattress. Started trusting the routine.

Morning workout. Forty minutes on the treadmill, weights after. The physical exertion clears his head, prepares him for another day in the hole. Shower. Breakfast—chicken and rice, same as always, but he's found ways to make it more palatable. Bit of the dried herbs from the greenhouse. Small victories.

The vitamin cocktail goes down easier now. His body has adjusted to the routine, to the isolation, to the underground existence. The headaches from the first week have faded. Sleep comes more naturally. Even the 4:00 PM procedures feel manageable.

Just another day.

Rick moves through equipment checks methodically. The monitors in the communications room display empty cells. Everything normal. The facility hums its usual mechanical rhythm—pipes dripping somewhere in the walls, ventilation system cycling, the constant white noise of machinery that's become almost comforting in its consistency.

"Morning, Rick." Lily's voice through the intercom sounds cheerful. "How did you sleep?"

"Not bad, actually. Getting used to things."

"That's wonderful to hear. I knew you'd adapt. You've got that military discipline—structure helps in a place like this."

Rick nods even though she can't see him. She's right. The structure does help. Knowing what each day will bring, what's expected, what needs to be done. No surprises. No variables.

"Today's Cell A at four," Lily continues. "Everything's running smoothly. Why don't you spend some time in the greenhouse this morning? The tomatoes are coming along beautifully. You've got a real talent for it."

Pride flickers in Rick's chest. Stupid to feel proud about growing tomatoes, but it's something. "Will do."

The greenhouse has become his sanctuary. The grow lights, the smell of earth and living things, the tangible progress of plants growing under his care. Rick checks the irrigation system—still dripping slightly near the valve, he really should tighten that—and examines each plant.

The basil is thriving. Tomatoes developing fruit. Even the temperamental peppers are producing. Rick prunes, waters, tends. His hands know the work now. No fumbling, no uncertainty.

Eight days. Just over a week underground, and it's starting to feel almost normal.

Days 9-15

The days blur together in a way that should be disturbing but isn't. Each morning the same. Each afternoon building toward 4:00 PM. Each evening cleanup and conversation with Lily.

Rick knows what he's cleaning now. Knows what's being fed to the specimen. Criminals, Lily said. Already deceased, repurposed for containment. The explanation should horrify him—does horrify him, when he lets himself think about it.

But he's learned not to think about it.

The procedures rotate through the cells—A, B, C, A, B, C— a pattern Rick can predict now. He knows which cells are louder, which feeding cycles run longer, how long each cleanup will take. The sounds from beyond the outer doors still disturb him, still remind him what he's actually doing here, but the edge of horror has dulled.

Adaptation. That's what Lily calls it. Rick calls it survival.

The conversations with Lily have settled into comfortable rhythm. She asks about his day, he reports on facility maintenance and the greenhouse. Sometimes they talk about other things—books they've read, music they miss, what they'll do after their contracts end. Nothing too deep. Nothing that requires vulnerability.

But it's human contact. It's company. And in the isolation of Threshold Station, that matters more than Rick wants to admit.

"You know what I miss most?" Lily says one evening during their check-in. "Rain. The sound of it on windows. The smell of it on pavement. Down here, everything's so controlled. No weather, no seasons, no natural rhythms. Just the facility and its schedules."

Rick understands that. Misses it too. "Summer storms in Surrey. Used to sit on the porch and watch them roll in. Lightning over the fields."

"That sounds lovely."

"It was."

Pause. Comfortable silence. Then Lily continues. "I'm glad you're here, Rick. I know that probably sounds strange, but it's true. You're different from most of the people who take this assignment. More resilient. More capable of handling what we do here."

The praise lands warm. "Thanks. I appreciate that."

"I mean it. We make a good team."

Rick finds himself smiling. "Yeah. I suppose we do."

The greenhouse leak persists. Rick notices it regularly now —puddle forming near the irrigation pipe—but it's not getting worse, so he keeps meaning to fix it and keeps forgetting. Other priorities. Other tasks. It's just condensation anyway. Nothing urgent.

By Day 15, Rick realizes he hasn't thought about the journal in over a week. The 1974 one sitting on his shelf. He'd meant to read it, kept meaning to, but there's been no time. No urgency. And honestly, he's not sure he wants to know what the previous occupant experienced.

Things are going well. Why complicate that with someone else's trauma?

Days 16-20

Week three brings subtle changes. Rick's muscles have adapted to the daily workouts—he increases the treadmill speed, adds more weight to his routine. His body is stronger than it's been in years. The physical labor of maintenance and cleanup provides constant exercise.

The food remains monotonous, but Rick's gotten creative. Tomatoes from the greenhouse add fresh acidity to the canned meals. Basil brightens everything. He's even started experimenting with the dried spices in storage, creating variations that make each meal feel less like survival rations.

Small victories. Small comforts.

The 4:00 PM procedures continue their rotation. Rick has developed efficient cleanup protocols for each cell. He knows which cleaning chemicals work best on which surfaces, how to angle the hose for maximum efficiency, where the blood tends to pool and requires extra attention.

Professional competence in a nightmare job.

Lily mentions it during one of their evening conversations. "Your cleanup times have improved significantly. Cell B used to take you nearly two hours. Now you're done in ninety minutes."

"Practice makes perfect."

"It certainly does. You've really mastered the routine here. I'm impressed."

Rick allows himself to feel that pride again. He's good at this. Despite the horror, despite the isolation, he's adapted and excelled. That has to count for something.

"Three weeks complete," Lily says on Day 20 evening. "How are you feeling about everything?"

Rick considers the question. Three weeks ago he'd been terrified, overwhelmed, questioning every choice that brought him here. Now?

"Honestly? I'm managing. Better than managing, actually. It's hard work, and it's disturbing, but it's also structured. Predictable. I can do this."

"I knew you could. From the moment you arrived, I could tell you were different. Special. The kind of person who can handle what we do here and come out stronger for it."

The words wrap around Rick like warmth. Special. Different. He wants to believe that. Needs to believe that after everything.

"Thanks, Lily. That means a lot."

"Get some rest. Tomorrow's Day 21. Three full weeks. You should feel proud of that."

The line clicks off.

Rick sits in his quarters, feeling unexpectedly content. Three weeks. Twenty-one days. And he's not just surviving—

he's thriving. The isolation that seemed unbearable at first has become manageable. The work that horrified him has become routine.

He can do this. Six months. Twenty-three weeks left. But if the first three are any indication, he'll make it through easily.

The journal on his shelf catches his eye. That 1974 date embossed on worn leather. Maybe he'll read it this weekend. Or next month. There's time.

So much time.

Rick lies down on the bed—mattress now, not floor—and closes his eyes. Sleep comes easily.

In the greenhouse, water continues seeping through the crack in the irrigation pipe. The seal weakens further. Pressure builds. But the leak is slow, gradual. Not urgent enough to warrant immediate attention.

Not yet.

Day 21 - 3:30 PM

The alarm sounds as usual. Rick's already in position, already prepared. Cell B today. He knows the routine by heart now.

"Ready?" Lily's voice comes through the intercom.

"Always am."

"Good. Standard protocol. Should be straightforward."

The clock ticks toward 4:00 PM. Rick watches the monitor displaying Cell B, hands relaxed on the desk edge. No tension now. No fear. Just another procedure.

4:00 PM.

The outer door of Cell B begins to open.

Then the facility shakes.

Not tremor. Not settling. A violent lurch that throws Rick against the desk, sends equipment crashing from shelves. The monitors flicker, go dark, then snap back on with distorted images.

"What the bloody hell—"

Alarms wail. Not the standard 3:30 PM warning, but something higher-pitched and urgent. Red emergency lighting kicks in, bathing everything in crimson. The facility groans around him—metal scraping stone, something deep underground straining against containment.

"Rick!" Lily's voice cuts through chaos, but there's static underneath. Words slightly delayed, tone strained. "Rick, stay calm. There's been a system malfunction. The feeding protocol is compromised."

Rick's training takes over. He grabs the desk to steady himself as another tremor hits. "What kind of malfunction?"

"The ceiling hatch in Cell B—it's not closing properly. Multiple subjects have been delivered." Pause, then urgency Rick has never heard from Lily before. "Rick, I need you to check the cell. Verify the outer door is still sealed."

Multiple subjects. Christ.

Rick spins toward the monitors, searching for the Cell B feed. The image flickers—distorted, pixelated, entire sections of the screen filled with static. He can make out movement, dark shapes, but nothing clear enough to confirm door status.

"The monitors," Rick says, voice tight. "They're not giving me a clear image. Too much interference."

"Damn it." Lily never curses. The fear in her voice makes Rick's chest tighten. "Rick, you need eyes on that cell. The cameras aren't reliable right now, and if that outer door is compromised—"

She doesn't finish the sentence. Doesn't need to.

Rick's already moving, stumbling down the corridor toward the cell blocks despite every instinct screaming at him to run the other direction. The facility protests around him—groaning metal, scraping stone, temperature dropping so fast his breath mists. Emergency lights strobe red, red, red.

The sound coming from Cell B stops him in his tracks.

Not just the usual feeding sounds. Screaming. Human screaming mixing with wet tearing, with impacts that shake the walls. Multiple voices—at least three, maybe more—overlapping in terror and agony.

Rick's hands shake as he reaches the observation window.

The cell is chaos.

Bodies scattered across the floor. Rick counts four—no, five—some still moving, trying to crawl away from the darkness spilling through the outer door. Blood covers every surface, sprays the walls in patterns suggesting desperate struggle. Fresh blood, still flowing.

And the specimen—

God.

Rick's mind can't process what he's seeing. The darkness isn't just absence of light. It's substance, form, something with presence and terrible intelligence. It writhes and pulses as it feeds, multiple appendages—or tentacles, or limbs, Rick can't tell—reaching for the bodies with deliberate hunger.

One of the subjects is still alive. Still screaming. Trapped in the corner, pressing against the wall as pale shapes wrap around their torso. The person fights—kicking, clawing, shrieking—but the appendages pull inexorably toward the outer door.

Rick watches, frozen, as the screaming figure disappears into darkness. The sound cuts off abruptly. Silence. Then wet tearing noises resume.

Rick's stomach heaves. He turns away, presses his back against corridor wall, forces himself to breathe.

"Rick?" Lily's voice crackles through the intercom. Static distorts her words. "Report."

"Multiple bodies." Rick's voice sounds distant even to himself. "At least four, maybe five. Some were..." He can't finish the sentence. Can't say *alive*. Can't acknowledge what he just witnessed.

"Bloody hell." Lily never curses. Never loses composure. But now her voice carries genuine fear. "Is the outer door still closed?"

Rick forces himself to look through the window again. The outer door is sealed now, darkness retreating behind it. But the cell is carnage. Bodies torn apart, blood pooling, viscera scattered across concrete.

"It's closed. Specimen is contained."

"Thank God." Lily's relief sounds authentic. Raw. "Rick, listen carefully. Do not enter that cell. Do not attempt cleanup yet. The facility needs time to stabilize. I'm reporting this to command. Just—stay in the communications room. I'll keep you updated."

Rick doesn't argue. Doesn't want to go near that cell anyway. He stumbles back toward the communications room, his mind replaying what he witnessed.

Multiple bodies. Living people fed to that thing. And Lily's genuine panic when she learned about the malfunction.

The comfortable routine of the past three weeks crumbles. The false security evaporates like morning fog. Rick has been lying to himself, pretending this is manageable, pretending he's adapted.

But adaptation was just denial. Routine was just avoidance.

And now he can't pretend anymore.

Rick collapses into the desk chair. The monitors flicker, showing distorted images of empty cells. Static crawls across screens. His hands won't stop shaking.

The intercom crackles. "Rick, I'm going to be off comms for the next few hours. Need to coordinate with command, figure out what caused the malfunction. Are you all right?"

No. He's not all right. Nothing about this is all right.

"I'm fine."

"Good. Stay in the communications room. Don't attempt any procedures until I give the all-clear. And Rick—you did well today. Stayed calm under pressure. That's exactly the kind of composure we need."

The praise rings hollow. Rick doesn't respond.

The line clicks off.

Silence settles over the facility. Emergency lighting fades back to normal fluorescents. As if the malfunction never happened. As if multiple people didn't just die screaming in Cell B.

Rick sits in the quiet, trying to process everything. Three weeks of building trust, of settling into routine, of convincing himself this was manageable—all of it shattered in fifteen minutes.

He'd been wrong. So fucking wrong.

This place isn't manageable. It's horror wearing the mask of routine. And he's been complicit in it, pretending professional competence made it acceptable.

The journal on his shelf flashes through Rick's mind. The previous occupant from 1974. Did they experience something like this? Did they have the same moment of realization—that adaptation was just self-deception?

Rick should read it. Should learn what happened to the person who lived here before. Should understand the pattern.

But not now. Now he needs to think. Needs to figure out what the hell he's actually doing here.

And whether he can continue doing it.

Day 22 - 6:00 AM

Rick didn't sleep. Couldn't sleep. Every time he closed his eyes, he saw the bodies in Cell B. Saw the person being dragged into darkness, still screaming. Heard the wet sounds that followed.

Morning routine provides structure despite exhaustion. Workout—pushing harder than usual, trying to burn out the images through physical pain. Shower. Breakfast.

But nothing feels normal anymore. The comfortable rhythm of the past three weeks is gone. Every sound in the facility makes Rick jump. Every shadow seems to move wrong. The walls feel closer, the air heavier.

He's on edge. Paranoid. Can't settle.

Lily checks in during his equipment inspection. "Morning, Rick. How did you sleep?"

Terrible question. "Not well."

"I understand. Yesterday was traumatic. But I want you to know—that kind of malfunction is extremely rare. In all my time here, I've never seen anything like it."

All her time. How long is that, exactly? Rick wants to ask but doesn't.

"What caused it?" he asks instead.

"We're still investigating. Some kind of failure in the hatch mechanism. The timing system malfunctioned, delivered multiple subjects before the previous cycle completed. It shouldn't have been possible."

Shouldn't have been. But it had happened. Rick saw it happen.

"Command is implementing new safety protocols," Lily continues. "Additional redundancies to prevent future incidents. You're safe, Rick. The facility is secure."

Safe. The word sounds absurd after yesterday. But Rick doesn't argue. Just nods even though she can't see him.

"Today we'll skip the procedure," Lily says. "Give you time to recover. The cleanup in Cell B can wait until tomorrow. Focus on maintenance, the greenhouse, whatever helps you process."

"Right. Thanks."

"And Rick? If you need to talk—about anything—I'm here."

The line clicks off.

Rick sits in silence, processing the conversation. Lily sounds genuine. Concerned. Like she actually cares about his wellbeing. But something about her responses feels practiced. Rehearsed. Like she's given this exact speech before.

How many people has she guided through this facility? How many have experienced similar incidents?

And why does she keep saying he's different, special, when she's probably said that to everyone who came before?

Rick's mind circles back to the journal. The 1974 one. Fifty-one years ago. Same facility, same procedures, probably same malfunctions.

Maybe it's time to stop avoiding it. Time to learn what happened to the person who stood where he's standing now.

But first, the greenhouse. Lily was right about that—tending the plants helps. Gives his hands something to do, his mind a distraction from yesterday's horror.

Day 22 - 10:00 AM

Rick enters the greenhouse and immediately notices the water.

Not just the usual puddle near the irrigation pipe. Actual flooding. Water covers the floor, soaking into the raised beds, pooling around the potting bench. The drip he's been ignoring for weeks has become a steady stream.

"Bollocks."

Rick moves to the irrigation valve, tries to shut it off. The handle turns but the water doesn't stop. The crack in the pipe has grown too large. Pressure keeps forcing water through the seal.

He needs tools. Needs to replace the entire valve section. This is beyond quick fixes.

Rick splashes back toward the storage area to gather supplies, but something catches his eye. The water isn't just pooling randomly. It's flowing. Moving with purpose across the floor, following a path that defies the slight slope of the greenhouse.

Flowing toward the back wall.

Rick follows the water, watches it reach the wall and then —impossibly—seep underneath. Through what looks like a hairline crack at the base. As if there's space behind the wall. Empty space where water can collect.

That's not right. The facility schematics don't show anything behind this wall. Just solid foundation, original Victorian-era construction.

So why is water flowing through it?

Rick presses his hand against the wall, feels slight vibration. Faint but present. Something beyond this barrier. Something active.

He knocks once, twice.

The sound that returns is hollow.

Definitely empty space back there.

Rick steps back, his mind racing. A hidden room. A section of the facility he hasn't been shown. Why? What's back there that needs to be concealed?

His training kicks in. If there's a hidden space, there must be an access point. A door, a panel, something that opens. Rick runs his hands along the wall, searching for seams, for any indication of how to get through.

There.

Near the floor, where the water is seeping through, Rick finds a section that gives slightly under pressure. Not a crack —a panel. Deliberately constructed to look like solid wall but actually designed to open.

Rick works his fingers around the edge, pulls. The panel resists at first, swollen from water damage, but finally gives. It swings open on corroded hinges, revealing darkness beyond.

A corridor. Narrow, unlit, but definitely intentional construction.

Rick retrieves his torch from the maintenance kit, shines it into the opening. The beam cuts through darkness, reveals stone walls and a passageway extending maybe ten metres before terminating at another door.

A hidden section of the facility. Concealed behind the greenhouse wall.

Rick's pulse quickens. He should report this to Lily. Should follow protocol. But something stops him. Some instinct that says if this room is hidden, there's a reason. And that reason might not be something Lily wants him to discover.

He checks the intercom panel in the greenhouse. No indicator light. No sign Lily is monitoring this area. The cameras in here are minimal—just one mounted near the entrance, covering the doorway but not the back wall.

Rick makes a decision.

He squeezes through the opening into the hidden corridor, torch beam leading the way. The air is colder here, stale with decades of being sealed. His footsteps echo off stone walls as he moves toward the door at the end.

The door is heavy wood, Victorian-era like the original facility construction. No lock. Just a simple handle. Rick turns it, pushes.

The door opens into a room.

And Rick stops breathing.

Day 22 - 10:15 AM - The Archive

* * *

The room is maybe four meters square. Stone walls, low ceiling, single electric light that flickers when Rick finds the switch. Not modern construction—this is original facility, from when Threshold Station was first excavated.

But it's been maintained. Recently. Everything is organized, catalogued, deliberately preserved.

Shelves line three walls, filled with filing boxes and binders. A small desk sits in the centre, surface clear except for a ledger lying open. And on the fourth wall—

Photographs. Dozens of them. Pinned to a bulletin board in neat rows.

Faces staring back at Rick. Men and women of various ages, various eras based on clothing and photo quality. Some black and white, some color, some recent enough to be digital prints. Each photograph labeled with a name and date.

Personnel records. Previous occupants.

Rick moves closer, his torch beam playing across the faces. So many people. Decades of people who stood where he's standing now, who worked in this facility, who fed the specimen and cleaned the cells and talked to Lily.

Thomas Morrison - 1923 Catherine Hughes - 1941 James Park - 1967 Sarah Mitchell - 1989 Simon Miller - 2015

The dates span over a century. And every face has the same expression—confident at first, deteriorating in later photos. The progression is visible. Hope to anxiety to desperation.

Some photos have notes attached. Brief comments in neat handwriting.

Thomas Morrison: Completed contract. Significant psychological trauma. Relocated to psychiatric care. Catherine Hughes: Requested early extraction after 73 days. Granted. James Park: Contract terminated due to mental breakdown. Extraction Day 134. Simon Miller: Completed contract. Subsequent whereabouts unknown.

Rick's hands shake as he processes what he's seeing. This

isn't just storage. This is documentation. Someone has been systematically recording every person who's worked here. Tracking their progress, noting their outcomes.

Studying them.

Rick moves to the shelves, pulls down the nearest filing box. Inside: personnel files. Detailed records of previous occupants. Medical history, psychological profiles, performance evaluations.

He opens one at random.

PERSONNEL FILE: DR. ELIZABETH CHEN Assignment: Threshold Station - Research Team Dates: March 1987 - June 1987 Role: Xenobiologist - Specimen Analysis

Initial Assessment: Dr. Chen brings extensive experience in anomalous biology. Her expertise in non-terrestrial life forms makes her ideal candidate for specimen research. Confident, methodical, scientifically rigorous.

Week 4 Report: Dr. Chen has begun comprehensive documentation of specimen behavior patterns. Initial observations suggest intelligence far exceeding previous estimates. She has requested additional monitoring equipment and extends research period.

Week 8 Report: Growing concern regarding Dr. Chen's psychological state. Reports obsessive focus on specimen, sleep deprivation, refusal to maintain proper distance during observations. Multiple safety protocol violations documented.

Week 12 Report: Dr. Chen claims specimen is "communicating" with her. Describes auditory phenomena not corroborated by recording equipment. Exhibits signs of severe psychological deterioration. Immediate extraction recommended.

Final Note: Contract terminated Day 89. Dr. Chen extracted to psychiatric facility. Subsequent diagnosis: acute paranoid psychosis with auditory hallucinations. Prognosis: poor. **Recommendation: Discontinue all research-focused assignments. Containment only.**

Rick sets the file aside, his chest tight. A research team. Scientists who tried to study the specimen. And they went mad.

He pulls another file.

PERSONNEL FILE: THRESHOLD STATION RESEARCH TEAM Assignment: June 1956 - August 1956 Personnel: Dr. Harold Morrison (Lead), Dr. James Webb, Dr. Patricia Sullivan, Technicians Anderson & Kowalski, Security Officer Drake

Mission Brief: Comprehensive analysis of specimen behavior, containment effectiveness, and potential applications. Team authorized for extended observation during feeding cycles.

Week 2 Report: Team making significant progress. Dr. Morrison notes specimen exhibits behavioral patterns suggesting sapience. Recommends expanded study.

Week 4 Report: Growing interpersonal tension among team members. Dr. Webb reports disturbing dreams. Technician Anderson requests transfer. Security Officer Drake cites "morale concerns."

Week 6 Report: Multiple team members report hearing voices during specimen feeding cycles. Dr. Morrison insists sounds are specimen-generated communication attempts. Others attribute to psychological stress. Team cohesion deteriorating rapidly.

Week 8 Report: CRITICAL INCIDENT. During feeding procedure, three team members entered Cell A without authorization. Security Officer Drake discovered them attempting to open the outer door "to make contact." All three unresponsive to verbal commands. Physical restraint required.

Final Note: Emergency extraction authorized. All team members exhibited signs of severe shared psychosis. Psychiatric evaluation revealed consistent delusions regarding specimen's nature and intent. **Recommendation: Multi-person staffing creates resonance effect. Proximity to specimen during active periods triggers collective psychological breakdown. IMPLEMENT ISOLATION PROTOCOLS. Single occupant model only.**

Rick's blood runs cold. Research teams tried to study the specimen. Multiple teams across decades. And studying it destroyed them. Made them hear things, see things, believe they could communicate with it.

The organization learned that understanding the specimen is more dangerous than containing it.

So they stopped trying. Stopped researching. Switched to single occupants who are kept focused only on routine maintenance, told just enough to comply but not enough to ask deeper questions.

Easier to control. Less likely to dig too deep. Less likely to go mad together.

Rick pulls more files, scans through decades of documentation. The pattern is consistent. Early teams— multiple staff members with various roles—all ended badly. Breakdowns, psychosis, incidents requiring emergency extraction.

Then the shift. Late 1980s, early 1990s. Single occupant model implemented. Containment only. No research. No analysis. Just feeding and maintenance.

And the outcomes improved. People completed contracts. Some struggled, some broke early, but the catastrophic incidents stopped.

Because ignorance is safer than knowledge.

Rick's hands shake as he processes the implications. Lily has been keeping him ignorant deliberately. Building routine, encouraging adaptation, discouraging questions—all calculated to prevent him from understanding too much.

Because understanding leads to madness.

He moves to the desk, examines the ledger lying open. Neat columns recording names, dates, duration of assignment, outcome.

The entries go back to 1884. One hundred forty-one years of operations. Rick flips backward through pages, scanning decades of entries, and notices something odd.

The early entries—1884 through the 1950s—list multiple names per assignment date. Teams. Research groups. "Dr. Morrison & Team (6 personnel)." "Whitmore/Sullivan/ Anderson Research Group." Assignments lasting weeks or months, outcomes varying: "All personnel extracted - psychiatric evaluation required." "Critical incident - team disbanded."

Then, around 1960, the format changes.

Single names. Single occupants. One person per assignment, isolated, performing maintenance rather than research. "Containment only" appears repeatedly in the notes column. And the catastrophic outcomes decrease—fewer "critical incidents," fewer emergency extractions.

They learned. Research teams went mad together, fed off each other's deterioration. So they switched to isolation. One person at a time, kept ignorant, focused only on routine.

Expendable workers cycling through an impossible job. But cycling alone now.

Next to many entries, notes in the "outcome" column:

Completed contract. Early extraction - psychological breakdown. Completed contract - subsequent whereabouts unknown. Terminated - critical incident.

Rick flips backward through pages, scanning decades of entries. The pattern repeats. Some people make it. Most don't. But the system continues, occupant after occupant, feeding the specimen, maintaining containment.

Then Rick sees something that makes his chest tighten.

On the shelf beside the desk: journals.

Not just a few. Dozens of them. Different sizes, different bindings, organized by date on multiple shelves. Personal records from previous occupants, systematically collected and archived.

Rick moves toward them, hand reaching for the nearest one. The leather is worn smooth by time, pages yellowed. He's about to pull it down when—

The intercom crackles to life. Static fills the small room.

"Rick?" Lily's voice, measured but with an edge underneath. "Where are you? I'm getting unusual readings from the greenhouse area."

Rick's pulse spikes. The journals sit on the shelf before him, untouched but tantalizingly close. All those decades of records. All those previous occupants. The pattern waiting to be discovered.

But Lily knows something's wrong.

Rick quickly steps away from the journals, leaves them exactly as he found them. His hands shake as he moves back toward the corridor. He has to make this look innocent. Just investigating the flood.

Rick moves quickly back toward the corridor, squeezes through into the greenhouse. Water still floods the floor, the irrigation pipe still leaking. But now the panel door stands open, obvious evidence of his discovery.

"Rick, please respond."

Rick keys his personal intercom. "Sorry, I'm here. Had a pipe burst in the greenhouse. Was trying to shut off the water."

Pause. Long enough that Rick's chest tightens.

"I see. And did you manage to fix it?"

"Working on it now. May need some parts from storage."

Another pause. Then Lily's voice, careful and deliberate: "Rick, were you able to explore the entire greenhouse? Sometimes flooding reveals unexpected structural issues."

She's giving him an out. A way to admit what he found without making it confrontational. But the careful phrasing tells Rick everything he needs to know.

She knows about the archive room. Knows what's in there. And she knows he's discovered it.

The question is: what happens now?

Rick makes a decision. "Actually, yeah. The flooding showed a panel that opened. Found a room back there. Old storage area, looks like. Full of files and... journals. Lots of journals."

Silence on the other end. Stretches so long Rick wonders if the connection has died.

Then: "I see. Rick, I think we should talk. Can you come to the communications room?"

It's not a request.

"On my way."

Rick leaves the greenhouse, his mind racing. Lily knows he's discovered the archive. Knows he's seen the personnel files, the research team reports, the journals spanning decades. Knows he understands the pattern.

What happens to occupants who learn too much?

He thinks about the files. The outcomes column. *Terminated - critical incident*. What does that mean, exactly?

Rick enters the communications room, approaches the intercom. His hands are steady despite the adrenaline coursing through his system. Military training surfaces—stay calm, assess situation, respond tactically.

"I'm here."

"Good." Lily's voice is different now. Still warm, still professional, but with an underlying tension Rick hasn't heard before. "I know you have questions. And you deserve answers. But first, I need to understand what you saw in that room. What you read."

Rick considers lying. Minimizing. But she already knows. Better to be direct.

"Personnel files. Research teams that went mad studying the specimen. Documentation showing this facility has operated for over a century with single occupants kept in the dark about its true history and purpose. And journals—dozens of them. Personal records from previous workers, all archived and organized."

"Did you read the journals?"

Rick hesitates. "No. I didn't have time before you called."

Long pause. He can almost hear her thinking through the intercom static.

Then Lily sighs. Long, almost weary. "I was hoping you wouldn't find that room at all. Most people don't. But you're more curious than average, more willing to investigate anomalies. I should have anticipated that."

"This facility has been operating since 1884. Over a hundred and forty years. And you never mentioned that."

"Would it have changed anything? You knew this was a classified government operation. Historical context isn't relevant to your assignment."

Rick's jaw tightens. Evasion. Always evasion. "The research teams," he presses. "The ones that went mad studying the specimen. What happened to them?"

"They learned things they shouldn't have. Saw patterns that damaged their perception of reality. The specimen isn't just a creature, Rick. It's something else. Something that affects people who try to understand it too deeply. The organization learned that containment requires ignorance. That questions lead to breakdown."

"So you keep us ignorant."

"I keep you safe. There's a difference."

"And the journals? Why collect them?"

"Understanding psychological progression helps us improve the system. Helps us identify people who might struggle before they break. It's not malicious—it's protective."

Rick's mind races, trying to piece together truth from careful evasion. "What happens now? Now that I know about the archive."

Long pause.

"That depends on you," Lily finally says. "Some people discover the archive and spiral. Can't handle knowing the history. Others process the information and continue working. The choice is yours."

"And if I can't continue?"

"Then we arrange extraction. You leave with compensation, sign an NDA, move on with your life. No one is forced to stay once they understand... enough."

The word hangs there. Enough. Not everything. Just enough.

"But Rick," Lily continues, her tone shifting to something firmer, "that room is off-limits now. You've seen what you've seen. Don't go back. The journals, especially—they're not meant for current occupants. Reading them causes more harm than good. The psychological contamination from previous workers' experiences is... significant."

"Psychological contamination."

"People project their fears into those journals. Their paranoia. Their delusions. Reading them spreads that mental deterioration. It's documented. It's why we seal that room. Do you understand?"

Rick's jaw tightens. She's warning him off. Which means there's something in those journals she doesn't want him to see.

"I understand."

"Good. Now—there's something else we need to discuss.

Tomorrow's procedure."

Rick's attention sharpens. "What about it?"

"I need to coordinate with command about yesterday's malfunction. Full system review, safety protocol updates. It's going to require my complete attention for most of the day. Which means I'll be offline during your four o'clock procedure."

Rick's chest tightens. "Offline?"

"You'll need to handle it alone. But you've done this before, Rick. You know the protocols. The system is automated—you just need to monitor and respond if anything goes wrong. Which it won't. We've implemented new redundancies."

Alone. The word echoes in Rick's mind. No Lily on the intercom. No guidance. No oversight.

Perfect opportunity to go back to the archive.

The thought surfaces unbidden, and Rick pushes it away. But it lingers.

"All right," Rick says carefully. "I can manage."

"I know you can. And Rick—I meant what I said. Stay out of that room. For your own psychological wellbeing. Promise me."

Rick hesitates. Making a promise feels like commitment. Like agreement to ignore what he's found.

"I need time," he says instead. "To process this. To figure out what I'm actually doing here."

"Take all the time you need. But Rick—consider this: the specimen must be contained. That's not manipulation or deception. It's reality. Whatever you think about me, about the facility, about the methods we use—containment is necessary. The alternative is worse. Much worse."

"How do you know?"

"Because I've seen what happens when containment fails."

The line clicks off before Rick can ask what she means.

Rick sits in the communications room, surrounded by dark

monitors and ancient equipment. The comfortable routine of the past three weeks has been replaced by something else. Questions. Suspicions. And a gnawing need to know what's in those journals.

Lily told him not to read them. Warned him away with talk of psychological contamination and documented harm.

Which means they contain something she doesn't want him to discover.

Rick thinks about tomorrow. Four o'clock procedure. Lily offline, coordinating with command. The archive room sitting empty behind the greenhouse wall, journals organized on shelves, decades of previous occupants' experiences waiting to be read.

He should stay away. Should follow her warning. Should focus on his job and stop digging into things that aren't his concern.

But Rick has never been good at leaving questions unanswered.

Day 22 - 11:00 PM

Rick lies in bed, staring at the ceiling. Sleep won't come. His mind keeps replaying the conversation with Lily. The archive. The personnel files showing 141 years of operation. The journals he glimpsed but didn't read.

The shelf above his bed catches his eye. The 1974 journal sits exactly where he left it three weeks ago.

Fifty-one years old. What did someone experience here half a century ago? Were the procedures the same? Did they clean the same cells, face the same horror?

Rick pulls it down, opens to a random middle page.

Week 7. Another day, another procedure. Cell B today. The cleanup took two hours. Standard protocol. Everything by the book.

Generic. Procedural. Nothing revealing.

He flips forward a few more pages.

Week 10. Routine maintenance on the greenhouse irrigation system. The basil is coming along well. Small victories.

Rick skips to near the end. Several pages are torn out—ragged edges where entries used to be. The final entry that remains is dated August 19th:

Day 186. Seven days left. Can't wait to get out of here. The isolation gets to you after a while.

Then nothing. Blank pages after that.

Rick closes the journal slowly. Same kind of work he's doing. Same facility maintenance, same procedures, same isolation. Nothing he doesn't already know. The missing final pages suggest Simon either destroyed them during his last week or the organization removed them when they archived his belongings.

But there's nothing here that explains the 141-year pattern. Nothing about how the facility has operated across generations, who ran it, why the procedures never changed.

The archive, though. The archive has dozens of journals spanning over a century. Personnel files documenting outcomes. Research team reports. That's where the real answers are. That's where he'll understand the full scope of whatever this place actually is.

Rick sets the journal back on the shelf. Tomorrow, when Lily's offline, he'll go to the archive. Read through the decades of records. See the complete picture, not just one person's incomplete experience.

That's where the truth is.

He lies back down. Sleep still won't come, but at least now he has a plan. Tomorrow he'll have answers.

And tomorrow, for the first time since arriving at Threshold Station, he'll be completely alone.

4

Day 23 - 7:00 AM

Rick didn't sleep well. Couldn't stop thinking about the journals. Dozens of them, sitting on those shelves in the archive room, waiting. Lily's warning echoed through his mind: *Don't go back. The journals, especially—they're not meant for current occupants.*

Which means they contain something she doesn't want him to see.

He goes through his morning routine mechanically. Workout. Shower. Breakfast. The vitamin cocktail tastes bitter today. Everything feels off, charged with anticipation. Today Lily will be offline. Today he'll have the archive to himself.

Today he'll learn the truth.

Rick checks the intercom at 8:00 AM. No morning check-in from Lily. She said she'd be coordinating with command most of the day, offline during his procedure. He's on his own.

Perfect.

He should prepare for the 4:00 PM feeding. Should run equipment checks, verify protocols, make sure everything is ready without Lily's guidance. That's the responsible choice. The professional choice.

But the journals pull at him. All morning, Rick tries to focus on other tasks. He tends the greenhouse—the irrigation leak is finally fixed, the cracked valve section replaced with a spare from storage and sealed tight with plumber's tape. He runs diagnostics on the communications equipment. He inventories cleaning supplies. Busy work. Distraction.

By noon, he can't take it anymore.

Rick stands in the greenhouse, staring at the back wall where the hidden panel waits. Lily explicitly told him not to go back. Warned him about psychological contamination, about previous occupants' paranoia spreading through their written words.

But if that were true, why archive the journals at all? Why organize them so carefully, preserve them for over a century? No—they're not just collecting data. They're hiding something.

And Rick needs to know what.

He checks his watch. 12:15 PM. Three hours and forty-five minutes until the procedure. Plenty of time to read a few journals and get back.

Rick opens the panel.

Day 23 - 12:20 PM - The Archive

The corridor is just as he left it. Cold. Stale air. The single light bulb in the archive room flickers when he switches it on, casting unstable shadows across the shelves.

The journals wait exactly where he saw them yesterday. Dozens of leather-bound volumes, organized chronologically. Rick moves to the nearest shelf, runs his fingers along the spines. Dates embossed in faded gold: 1974. 1984. 1989. 1997. 2003. 2015.

One hundred forty-one years of previous occupants. One

hundred forty-one years of experiences, observations, deterioration.

One hundred forty-one years of whatever truth Lily doesn't want him to find.

Rick pulls down the 1974 journal—the same date as the one on his shelf in his quarters. The one he glanced at last night before deciding the archive would have more comprehensive evidence.

But as he opens this one, something strikes him immediately.

The pages are too clean. Too uniform. This isn't an original journal—it's a photocopy. Professional quality, bound to look like the real thing, but definitely reproduced. The handwriting is there, but it's flat, lacking the indentations and ink variations of actual writing.

Rick's chest tightens. They photocopied all the journals. Which means the originals exist somewhere—or existed. The one in his quarters is an original. Left there deliberately, as he realized yesterday. But why leave an original while keeping copies in the archive?

Unless they edited the copies. Removed certain pages. Redacted specific entries.

Rick examines the photocopied journal more closely. Clean, complete, but sanitized. The organization controls what information reaches current occupants through these archived copies.

The original on his shelf might contain more. Might have entries they didn't want preserved in the official record.

He should go get it. Compare them directly. See what—if anything—was removed.

But there are dozens of journals here. All showing the pattern across decades. That's more important right now. He needs to see the full scope first. Understand what they've been hiding for over a century.

He'll compare them later. After he understands what he's dealing with. The original isn't going anywhere—it's been sitting in his quarters for three weeks already.

Rick opens the photocopied 1974 journal.

January 15, 1974

First day underground. The descent took forever. The coordinator seems professional enough over the intercom. Says she'll help me settle in. Christ, this place is isolated. But the pay is worth it. Six months. I can do six months.

Rick flips forward. February. March. The handwriting stays neat, controlled.

March 3, 1974

Getting used to the routine now. The 4 PM procedures are disturbing, but the voice on the intercom talks me through each one. She's good at that—making it feel manageable. Says I'm adapting well. Better than most people who take this assignment.

Better than most. Rick's stomach tightens. He's heard that phrase before.

April 18, 1974

Had a rough day. The cleanup in Cell B was worse than usual. The coordinator checked in on me afterward. We talked for almost an hour. She really understands what this isolation does to you. Makes me feel less alone down here. She says there's something different about me. Something resilient.

(Note: 15:47:23 / 52.8765°S, 68.2154°W / CONVERGENCE POINT?)

Rick pauses. That's odd. The note doesn't match the rest of the entry's tone. Coordinates and a timestamp? Why would someone be recording those in a personal journal?

He continues reading.

May 12, 1974

Three months complete. The woman on the communications system says I'm handling this better than she expected. That I'm special. That we're in this together.

(17:33:09 - CELLULAR SYNCHRONIZATION - ALL ITERATIONS SIMULTANEOUS)

More strange notations. Rick frowns. The writer's mental state must have been deteriorating even while he thought he was adapting. Random numbers and phrases scattered through otherwise coherent entries. Classic sign of psychological breakdown—the mind trying to impose pattern on chaos.

Rick sets the 1974 journal aside, pulls down 1997. Flips to a middle entry.

Day 47 - 1997

The coordinator and I have gotten close. Is that weird to say about someone you've never met face-to-face? But our evening conversations are the only thing keeping me sane. She says I'm special. That I'm handling this better than previous occupants. That we're in this together.

We're in this together.

The same phrase. Rick's hands shake slightly. He grabs the 2003 journal.

Week 9 - 2003

I look forward to talking with Lily more than anything else. She gets it. Gets what it's like down here. The isolation, the horror of what we do at 4 PM, all of it. She says I'm different from the others. More capable. More resilient.

Rick freezes.

Lily.

The 2003 journal writer called the coordinator Lily.

That's... that's his coordinator's name. The woman who's been talking to him for three weeks. The one who makes him feel special. Different. Capable.

His chest tightens. Could be coincidence. Common enough name. Different coordinator, same name. The organization probably cycles through staff. That happens.

But the phrases. "I'm different from the others." "More

capable." "More resilient."

The exact same words Rick's heard. The exact same script his Lily uses.

Rick's hands shake as he pulls down another journal. 2007. Flips through entries desperately.

Day 31 - 2007

Lily says I'm handling this better than she expected. That I'm special. That we're in this together.

There it is again. Lily.

Same name. Same phrases. 2007.

Rick's breathing quickens. He grabs 2015. The David Chen journal. Scans frantically for the name.

Day 18 - 2015

Had another long conversation with Lily tonight. She's the only thing keeping me sane down here. Says there's something different about me. Something resilient.

No. No, this can't be right.

Rick pulls journals frantically now. 1989. 1992. 1999. 2010. His hands shake so badly he drops one, has to pick it up. Different handwriting, different dates, different people.

But the same name. Over and over.

Lily. Lily. Lily.

She says I'm not like the previous occupants.

She says there's something about me.

She says we're in this together.

Different handwriting. Different years. Different people.

But the same name. The same script. The same manipulation.

Every journal. Every occupant. Every worker who descended into this facility thinking they were starting a new assignment.

All of them talking to Lily.

All of them hearing the same lies.

All of them made to feel special, different, chosen.

Rick's mind flashes back to those strange notations. The coordinates. He grabs the David Chen journal again—the 2015 occupant. Flips to the entries with the cryptic notes.

Day 52 - 2015

Can't sleep. Dreaming about Cell A. Same dream every night. I'm inside it, paralyzed, and something's coming through the outer door. I try to move, try to scream, but I'm frozen.

Lily says it's just stress. Says I'm different from the previous occupants. That I'm handling it better.

(CRITICAL: 16:00:00 EXACTLY - OUTER DOOR OPENS - MOMENT OF CONSUMPTION - THIS IS WHEN ALL POINTS CONVERGE)

There. The same kind of cryptic annotations from the 1974 journal. Timestamps. Phrases about convergence.

He flips to another entry.

Day 38 - 2015

Another feeding today. Cell A. The sounds from beyond the outer door are getting worse. Or maybe I'm just noticing them more. Lily says it's normal adaptation.

(NOTE: 52.8765°S, 68.2154°W / THRESHOLD COORDINATES / REMEMBER THIS)

The exact same coordinates from 1974. Forty-one years apart. Two different people, both recording identical information. Both experiencing something that made them document the same timestamps, the same coordinates, the same cryptic references.

Both talking to Lily.

Rick sets down the Chen journal. He can't process what the coordinates mean right now. He needs to check the original journal in his quarters later—see if these notations are real or if the organization added them to the archive copies.

Right now, he needs to understand the scope of this.

Rick's back hits the shelves. His mind races. How many coordinators could there be? How many different women named Lily working this facility over the decades?

Or—

No. That's not possible.

Rick's breathing quickens. He moves along the shelves, looking for older journals. If it's the same coordinator using the same name, the same script on recent occupants, how far back does it go?

He grabs the oldest journal he can read clearly. 1922. The handwriting is formal, stilted, but he forces himself to focus.

15th November, 1922

Thank providence for Miss Lily and our evening conversations. The isolation weighs heavier each day, but she possesses a remarkable understanding of the human condition. She claims I exhibit unusual fortitude. That I am unlike those who preceded me in this assignment.

Rick's stomach drops. 1922. Over a hundred years ago.

And the coordinator was named Lily.

But people don't work the same job for over a hundred years. Don't maintain the same position, the same role, across generations.

Unless—

He reaches for an earlier journal. 1915. His hands tremble as he opens it.

Week 7 - 1915

Miss Lily on the speaking device provides my only comfort. She says I'm stronger than the others. More capable of handling the necessary procedures. That I'm special.

That I'm special.

The same words. The same manipulation. In 1915.

Rick's breath comes in short gasps. He grabs another. 1903.

Day 42 - 1903

The woman on the communication device—Lily, she calls herself—claims I possess qualities previous workers lacked. That I am different. More resilient. We are in this together, she says.

We're in this together.

Rick's vision blurs. The journals scatter as he reaches for the oldest one on the shelf. 1884. The facility's first year of operation. His hands shake so badly he can barely open it.

3rd March, 1884

Three months in this godforsaken hole. The loneliness gnaws at me. But the woman on the speaking device—she calls herself Lily—provides some solace. She claims I possess qualities the previous workers lacked. That I am stronger. More capable.

The same script. The same phrases. The same voice.

For one hundred forty-one years.

Rick drops the journal. His back hits the cold stone wall. The archive room spins around him—shelves packed with decades of journals, all containing the same manipulation, the same lies, the same performance.

Lily's been here since the beginning. Since the facility opened in 1884. Not a succession of different coordinators. Not a position passed down through generations.

The same Lily.

For one hundred forty-one years.

Rick's mind races. How? People don't live that long. Don't maintain the same job, the same voice, the same perfect script across more than a century.

She's not human. Can't be.

But what is she?

The realization sits in his chest like ice. Every conversation he's had with her. Every moment of comfort she provided. Every word of praise that made him feel special, different, capable—it was all performance. A script perfected over 141 years. Tested and refined on dozens of isolated workers who all thought they were unique.

All of them fed the same lines.

All of them manipulated the same way.

All of them ending up in these journals, their experiences

archived and sanitized for the next victim.

Rick forces himself to breathe. He can't process what she is right now. Can't answer questions he doesn't have information to solve. But he knows one thing with absolute certainty:

She's been lying to him since day one.

And she's been manipulating workers like him for 141 years.

Rick's watch shows 2:45 PM. He needs to focus. Still over an hour until the procedure. He should go back, get ready, but—

His eyes land on a red folder tucked behind the journals on the lowest shelf, partially hidden. The label reads: **CONTAINMENT BREACH PROTOCOLS - CLASSIFIED**.

Rick pulls it out. The folder is thick, filled with incident reports spanning decades. His hands shake as he opens it.

INCIDENT REPORT: March 15, 1973 Facility: Threshold Station

Occupant: Marcus Webb

Summary: Subject failure to monitor 4:00 PM procedure due to illness. Automated systems initiated feeding cycle without human oversight. Ceiling hatch malfunction resulted in premature subject delivery (3:57 PM). Outer door opened on schedule (4:00 PM) while subject remained conscious and mobile.

Outcome: Subject escaped Cell B containment, accessed main corridor. Occupant Webb failed to initiate emergency lockdown protocol from communications room. Contact with specimen resulted in complete facility contamination. Occupant Webb found deceased in quarters, cause undetermined. Specimen required 72 hours to return to dormant state. Facility remained sealed for decontamination.

Recommendation: Mandatory human oversight during ALL procedures. No exceptions. Occupant must remain at communications console to initiate manual containment override if automated systems fail.

Rick's blood runs cold. He flips to another report.

INCIDENT REPORT: August 8, 1996

Facility: Threshold Station Occupant: James Park

Summary: Occupant Park absent from communications room during 4:00 PM procedure (location: greenhouse). No human monitoring of cell operations. Multiple system malfunctions detected post-procedure. Investigation revealed outer door of Cell A remained partially open for 7 minutes beyond standard duration. No manual override initiated due to occupant absence.

Outcome: Specimen exhibited increased activity levels for 48 hours following incident. Occupant Park extracted Day 89 due to severe psychological deterioration. Medical examination revealed physiological changes consistent with prolonged specimen exposure.

Recommendation: Reinforce protocol adherence. Human oversight during procedures is CRITICAL to containment integrity. Manual override capability exists for a reason—it must be available to use.

More reports. 1989. 2001. 2008. Each one documenting what happens when procedures run without proper monitoring. Malfunctions. Contamination events. Specimen escaping containment boundaries. Occupants dying or deteriorating rapidly after exposure.

The procedures require human oversight. Not for the occupant's safety—for containment itself. Someone has to monitor, verify, respond immediately if anything goes wrong. Without that, the systems fail. And when the systems fail—

Rick thinks about Day 21. The malfunction that dropped five people into Cell B. Lily had responded immediately, warned him, kept him in the communications room monitoring every second. The outer door had held that time, but if it hadn't—if he'd needed to trigger that manual override—

The folder trembles in Rick's hands. These reports document decades of near-disasters. All because someone wasn't watching. All because the automated systems operated without human verification.

And today, Lily is offline. She won't be monitoring during the 4:00 PM procedure.

Which means Rick needs to be there. In the communications room. Watching every second. Ready to respond if something goes wrong.

He's not entirely sure what he'd do if the containment failed. The reports mention manual overrides, emergency lockdowns, protocols he's never been fully trained on. But the pattern is clear: presence matters. Being at that console, watching those monitors, having hands on the controls— that's the difference between incidents that get contained and incidents that end in death.

Rick gathers the breach reports, ready to take them back. Evidence of what happens when procedures run without oversight. He needs to get to the communications room, make sure he's ready for 4:00 PM.

The alarm cuts through the archive room. High-pitched, urgent.

Rick freezes. No. That can't be right.

He checks his watch. 3:30 PM.

Over three hours. Three and a half hours lost to journals and revelations and—

The procedure. Lily's offline. He has to monitor it alone.

And he just read a dozen reports showing exactly what happens without human oversight.

A mechanical grinding sound. Sharp. Immediate. Metal on metal.

Rick spins toward the corridor entrance.

The steel plate drops from the ceiling like a guillotine blade.

Rick runs.

The barrier slams into place with a sound like thunder. He crashes into cold steel a second too late, pounds his fists against the impenetrable surface.

"Open! Bloody hell, open!"

The metal doesn't budge.

The breach reports slip from his hands, scatter across the stone floor. Marcus Webb. James Park. Every incident that ended with containment failure started the same way.

Absent occupant. No oversight.

Rick's watch shows 3:32 PM. Twenty-eight minutes until the feeding begins.

He stares at the sealed barrier. At the stone walls. At one hundred forty-one years of journals documenting workers who learned the truth too late.

He's trapped.

5

The steel barrier stares back at Rick. Twenty-eight minutes until the procedure begins. Twenty-eight minutes to get from this sealed archive room to the communications room, or the feeding happens without oversight.

The breach reports at his feet document what happens when procedures run unmonitored.

"Open!" Rick slams his fists against metal. "Bloody hell, open!"

Nothing. Solid steel, emergency lockdown protocol. No handle on this side. No manual override. Just cold metal between him and his job.

Rick's breathing quickens. 3:33 PM. Twenty-seven minutes.

The archive room presses in. Stone walls, low ceiling, shelves packed with documentation. One hundred forty-one years of previous occupants who all made the same mistakes, trusted the same lies, fell for the same manipulation.

And now he'll join them. Not broken by the horror. Not destroyed by The Anomaly. Just curious at the worst possible time.

No. Rick forces himself to breathe. Think. There has to be another way out.

He examines the barrier again. No gaps, no seams. Solid construction, probably two inches thick. He's not breaking through this.

The walls then. Rick moves along the perimeter, pressing against stone. But this is original Victorian construction. Nothing gives.

3:35 PM. Twenty-five minutes.

Rick's pulse hammers. The breach reports mentioned contamination events, specimen escaping boundaries, occupants dying when procedures ran without oversight. One report detailed how an absent worker resulted in facility-wide lockdown lasting seventy-two hours.

He has to get out. Has to monitor the procedure. Has to—

His boot catches on something. Rick stumbles, catches himself against a shelf. The impact sends files cascading to the floor. Decades of personnel records scatter across stone.

And behind where the files were stacked—

A ventilation grate.

Rick's chest tightens. The grate is small, maybe sixty centimeters square, mounted low on the wall behind the shelf. Corroded screws hold it in place. The metal looks old enough to be original facility construction.

3:37 PM. Twenty-three minutes.

Rick grabs the shelf and pulls. Heavy. Solid wood, decades of files. But adrenaline makes him strong. The shelf screeches across stone, toppling forward. More files spill everywhere.

The ventilation grate waits behind it.

Rick drops to his knees, examines the screws. Rusted through in places, but still holding. He needs tools. His fingers won't—

Rick pats his pockets. Torch. Watch. Nothing else.

The desk. There's a letter opener on the desk, holding down a stack of photographs. Rick scrambles for it, returns to the grate, wedges the blade under a screw head.

The metal protests. Rust flakes shower down. The screw turns.

3:39 PM. Twenty-one minutes.

Rick works frantically, attacking each screw. His hands shake. The opener slips twice, gouging his palm. He doesn't stop. Can't stop.

First screw out. Second. Third.

The fourth strips completely, head shearing off. Rick swears, wedges the opener behind the grate itself, pulls. The remaining screws groan. The grate bends outward.

3:42 PM. Eighteen minutes.

One more pull. The grate tears free with a screech of metal.

Darkness yawns behind it. A ventilation shaft, narrow and pitch black. Rick can't see where it leads. Can't see if it's even large enough.

But it's the only option.

Rick shoves his torch through first. The beam cuts through decades of accumulated dust and grime. The shaft runs horizontal for maybe three meters, then branches. He can see junctions, other passages. A maze of ducts snaking through the facility's infrastructure.

Somewhere in there is a path to the communications room.

3:43 PM. Seventeen minutes.

Rick squeezes into the opening. His shoulders barely fit, scraping against corroded metal. The shaft is tight enough that he has to crawl on his belly, pulling himself forward with his forearms. No room to turn. No room to do anything except drag himself forward inch by painful inch.

The torch beam bounces ahead. More duct, more darkness. The metal groans under his weight. Rust flakes rain down, getting in his eyes, his mouth.

Keep moving. Just keep moving.

Rick reaches a junction. The passage continues straight ahead, or branches left. He doesn't know which leads to the communications room. Doesn't know the facility's layout well enough to navigate by ventilation alone.

3:48 PM. Twelve minutes.

The torch beam plays across each passage. Straight continues the same direction—that would take him parallel to where he came from. Left branches toward where he thinks the communications room should be.

Left. Has to be left.

Rick pulls himself into the left shaft. This one is even tighter. He has to drag himself forward inch by inch. The metal edges cut through his jacket, scraping his ribs. Blood makes his palms slippery.

Another junction. Another choice. Rick's mind races. The communications room is near his quarters. His quarters are adjacent to the greenhouse. The greenhouse was where he found the archive entrance.

So he needs to move toward—

There. Faint light bleeding through another grate ahead. Rick crawls faster. The shaft widens slightly as he approaches. He can see through the grate now into familiar space.

The communications room.

3:56 PM. Four minutes.

Rick reaches the grate. The opening is on the side of the shaft, about a meter before the duct dead-ends. He shoves against it. The screws hold.

Rick tries to turn his body in the confined space, but there's barely room to breathe, let alone maneuver. He manages to get onto his side, spine pressed against one wall, knees bent awkwardly against the other. The position is agonizing—his neck craned at a painful angle, his shoulders jammed into the metal seams. He draws his legs up as far as the cramped space allows and kicks at the grate.

The impact is weak. Wrong angle. He can barely generate

force in this contorted position.

Again. His hip screams in protest. The grate rattles but holds.

Rick sucks in a breath, tasting rust and old dust. One more try. He coils as much as the shaft allows and kicks with both feet.

The grate tears free on the third kick, clattering to the floor below.

Rick doesn't hesitate. He angles himself toward the opening—a painful process of squirming and scraping against corroded metal—and drops through. Hits the floor hard. His ankle protests. Dust covers him head to toe. Blood streaks his hands from the sharp metal.

But he's here. He's in the communications room.

3:58 PM.

Rick stumbles to the console, falls into the chair. His hands shake as he activates the monitors. The screens flicker to life. The three cells. All doors closed. Everything in position.

The clock reads 3:59 PM.

Rick forces himself to breathe. Made it. Barely, but made it. He wipes blood from his palms onto his trousers, grips the desk edge.

The alarm sounds. Thirty seconds.

Rick stares at the monitor showing Cell A. His heart hammers. The facility hums around him, machinery spinning up for the daily procedure.

4:00 PM.

The outer door of Cell A begins to open.

And everything goes wrong.

The facility doesn't just shake. It convulses. Rick grips the desk as the entire structure lurches. The monitors flicker violently. Half go dark. Emergency lighting kicks in. Everything bathes in red.

The sound from Cell A makes Rick's blood freeze.

Not the usual feeding sounds. Not wet tearing or organic crunching. This is something else. A roar that rattles Rick's teeth, reverberates through stone and metal and bone. The frequency is wrong. Too low for human hearing but his body feels it anyway.

The remaining monitors show chaos. The darkness spilling from the outer door isn't passive. It's aggressive. Writhing. Slamming against the walls hard enough to crack concrete. Rick watches as the cell camera shakes so violently the image becomes meaningless.

Something screams. Multiple somethings. Sounds layering over each other in ways that shouldn't be possible from a single source.

The facility groans. Actually groans. Like a ship taking on water. Rick hears metal warping, stone cracking. Somewhere in the depths, something massive shifts position.

The lights flicker, then go out completely. For three endless seconds, Rick sits in absolute darkness while the sounds continue.

Then emergency power kicks in. The monitors return. Distorted. Wrong. Static crawls across every screen. The timestamp in the corner glitches. Numbers scrambling.

Rick white-knuckles the desk edge. Forces himself to keep watching. This is his job. Monitor. Report. Respond if needed.

But there's nothing he can do. Nothing anyone can do. The procedure runs on automatic systems he doesn't control. All he can do is witness.

Fifteen minutes. The longest fifteen minutes of Rick's life.

When the outer door finally begins to close, the facility is still shaking. The monitors show Cell A in ruins. Walls gouged. Floor cracked. The reinforced outer door dented from inside.

And blood. So much blood.

The door seals with a heavy clang. The shaking subsides.

Emergency lighting fades back to normal fluorescents. The monitors stabilize. Static clearing.

Silence.

Rick sits in the chair, drenched in sweat despite the cold. His hands won't stop trembling. That was—

Christ. That was worse than anything he's witnessed. Worse than the Day 21 malfunction. Worse than finding the human ear. That was The Anomaly at its most active, its most aggressive, its most hungry.

And he'd almost missed it. Almost left it unmonitored.

The intercom crackles. "Rick?" Lily's voice. Calm. Professional. "How did it go?"

Rick's throat is too dry to respond immediately. He swallows. Forces words out. "Fine. Everything's fine. Standard procedure."

The lie comes easily. Automatically. Because what's he supposed to say? That he was trapped in the facility's hidden archive reading about her 141-year manipulation? That he discovered she's been using the same script on isolated workers since 1884? That he barely made it back in time and the procedure was the most violent thing he's ever witnessed?

"Good," Lily responds. Warmth returns to her voice. "I'm glad you handled it well. The system showed some minor fluctuations, but nothing concerning. You did exactly what you needed to do."

She doesn't know. Rick realizes the archive room must have no camera coverage—makes sense for a hidden space meant to store sensitive documentation. She didn't see him discover the journals, didn't see him get trapped, didn't see him crawl through the ventilation system covered in blood and rust. As far as Lily knows, Rick spent the day doing routine maintenance while she coordinated with command.

"Right," Rick manages. "No problems here."

"Excellent. I'll let you handle the cleanup. We can check in this evening."

The line clicks off.

Rick sits in the silence. Surrounded by flickering monitors. The lingering smell of ozone. She doesn't know. He could pretend nothing happened. Could continue the assignment as if he never discovered the truth.

But he can't forget what he learned. Can't unsee those journals, those personnel files, that ledger documenting 141 years of the same pattern repeating.

Lily has been here since the beginning. Has been manipulating facility occupants for over a century. Has been using the exact same phrases, the same psychological techniques, the same false intimacy on dozens—maybe hundreds—of isolated workers.

And she's doing it to him right now.

Rick thinks about their conversations. The ones where she opened up about her time at the facility. About understanding isolation. Were those even real? Or just practiced anecdotes, tested and refined over decades of use?

"You're different from the others." That's what she said. That's what she's said to everyone.

Rick closes his eyes. Four months left. One hundred twenty days of procedures and cleanup and conversations with someone who's been perfecting her lies since before his grandfather was born.

He could request extraction. The personnel files documented early departures—occupants who couldn't handle it, who demanded to leave before their contracts ended. Catherine Hughes made it seventy-three days. James Park lasted until Day 134.

But extraction means admitting failure. Means questions he doesn't want to answer, debriefings he doesn't want to endure. And truthfully, part of him needs to understand what's actually happening here. Walking away now, with partial knowledge—that would be worse than staying.

So he'll stay. He has to stay. See this through to whatever end awaits him.

But knowing what he knows now, how is he supposed to talk to her? How is he supposed to pretend their conversations are genuine when he's read the script she follows?

Rick looks down at himself. Blood on his hands from the vent crawl. Dust covering his clothes. Torn jacket.

Right. Clean up first. Then the cell.

Rick moves to the bathroom. Strips off his jacket. Washes the blood from his hands and face. Changes into clean clothes. The physical routine helps. Gives his mind something simple to focus on.

Then the cleanup beckons. Cell A waits. Blood-soaked and ruined. Rick forces himself to stand. To move toward the cell blocks.

Just do the job. Don't think. Don't feel. Just survive.

Days 24-34

Rick stops answering Lily's evening check-ins.

Not completely. He still responds to procedural communications. Acknowledges instructions. Confirms completion of tasks. Reports maintenance issues. But the personal conversations, the casual exchanges that made isolation bearable—those he cuts off.

When Lily asks how he's doing, Rick responds with single words. "Fine." "Managing." "Busy."

When she tries to engage him in conversation—asking about the greenhouse, about what he's reading, about how he's handling the isolation—Rick deflects. "Focused on work."

"Lots to do." "Not much to report."

He can hear the concern in her voice growing with each failed attempt at connection. But he can't engage. Can't pretend their relationship is real when he knows it's just a century-old script she's following.

At first, Rick tries to rationalize what he discovered. Maybe "Lily" is just a codename, a role passed down through generations of coordinators. Different women trained to use the same phrases, follow the same psychological playbook, maintain the same persona for continuity. The organization could have institutionalized the manipulation—a standard operating procedure refined over 141 years.

But the more he thinks about it, the less that explanation holds. The phrasing isn't just similar—it's identical. Word for word, across decades. "You're different from the others." "There's something about you." "We're in this together." No two people would deliver those lines exactly the same way for over a century. No training program could produce that level of consistency.

And then there's her voice. Rick has heard recordings from different eras during his surveillance reviews. The 1970s footage, the 1990s logs, the recent procedures. The voice quality changes with the recording technology, but the voice itself—the cadence, the warmth, the particular way she emphasizes certain words—it's the same. Not similar. The same.

One Lily. For 141 years.

Which means she's not human. Can't be.

Every warm word is borrowed from someone else's manipulation. Every moment of seeming connection is a technique she's perfected on dozens of workers before him.

The isolation crushes down harder than ever. Rick had thought he understood loneliness during his first weeks at the facility. But that was before he had Lily's voice to break the silence. Before he'd grown dependent on their evening conversations.

Now, cutting himself off from even that artificial connection, Rick discovers a new depth of solitude. The facility's silence becomes oppressive. The walls press closer. Time stretches and warps in ways that make him question whether days are actually passing or if he's just cycling through the same twenty-four hours on repeat.

He tries to fill the void with work. Maintenance tasks that don't need doing. Equipment checks performed three times daily. Excessive time in the greenhouse, pruning plants that don't need pruning, adjusting irrigation systems that function perfectly well.

But activity can't replace human connection. Rick finds himself talking aloud just to hear a voice—even if it's his own. Conducting entire conversations with imaginary versions of Lily, or his ex-girlfriend, or commanding officers from his military days. Sometimes he'll catch himself mid-sentence and realize he's been speaking to empty air for several minutes. Standing in the greenhouse explaining his situation to the tomato plants, asking the basil for advice.

It's absurd and he knows it. But it helps. Helps to speak aloud, to organize thoughts into words even if the audience can't respond.

The nightmares intensify. Every night now, without exception. The same dream: trapped in Cell A, body paralyzed, unable to move as the outer door begins to open. The darkness spills toward him and he can't even scream. Can only lie there, frozen, watching it come.

He wakes gasping, drenched in sweat, uncertain for several seconds whether he's in his quarters or actually in the cell. The line between nightmare and reality blurs.

Rick's physical condition deteriorates. His clothes hang looser now, several kilos lost to stress and reduced appetite.

The canned meals taste like ash. He forces himself to eat enough to maintain function, but nothing more. The vitamin cocktail becomes his primary nutrition.

Sleep deprivation makes everything worse. Rick averages maybe four hours per night, and those hours are fragmented by nightmares. Dark circles hollow out under his eyes. His hands develop a persistent tremor that makes equipment work more difficult.

The morning workouts become punishing rather than energizing. Rick pushes himself until his muscles scream, trying to exhaust his body enough that sleep might come easier. It doesn't work. Just leaves him physically depleted on top of mentally exhausted.

Lily keeps trying. Every few days, she attempts to break through his wall of professional distance.

"Rick, I'm concerned about you. Your vital signs show increased stress. Are you sleeping?"

"Enough."

"Your caloric intake has dropped significantly. Are you eating properly?"

"Managing."

"Rick, please. Talk to me. I know something's wrong. I can help if you let me."

He wants to scream at her. Wants to demand she explain how she's been here for 141 years. Wants to throw the journals at her, make her account for every lie, every manipulation, every person she's used this same script on.

But he doesn't. Because confrontation would require engagement, and engagement would require him to acknowledge how much he'd come to depend on her voice.

Better to maintain distance. Better to pretend she's just his supervisor and nothing more. Better to survive these last four months without emotional entanglement.

Even though isolation is killing him slowly.

The procedures continue their rotation. Cell A, Cell B, Cell C. Rick performs each one with mechanical precision. Monitors from the communications room. Watches the outer doors open and darkness spill through. Witnesses the feeding. Waits the required time. Performs cleanup.

The cleanup times improve despite his deteriorating condition. Muscle memory and practice make him efficient. He can strip a cell clean in under an hour now, removing every trace of violence, restoring everything to sterile neutrality.

Professional competence in a nightmare job. Rick clings to that. At least he's good at something.

But every time he descends into a blood-soaked cell, every time he hoses down walls and watches pink water spiral down drains, he thinks about the journals. About the workers who did this before him. About how they all followed the same pattern: arrival, adaptation, discovery, deterioration, disappearance.

He's in the deterioration phase now. Rick recognizes that. Can feel himself sliding toward whatever comes next in the cycle.

And he has no idea how to stop it.

By Day 32, Rick realizes he's losing weight too quickly. His trousers need a belt now to stay up. His shirt collars hang loose. When he catches his reflection in the bathroom mirror, the face staring back looks gaunt. Haunted.

He forces himself to eat more. Chokes down extra portions despite his stomach's protests. Takes the vitamin supplements religiously. Tries to maintain some baseline of physical health even as his mental state crumbles.

The isolation gnaws at him constantly now. Rick finds himself standing at the intercom panel multiple times each day, hand hovering over the call button, desperately wanting to reach out to Lily.

But he doesn't. Because he knows what she is. Knows that every word of comfort would be calculated, every moment of connection would be manipulation.

Even though he needs it anyway.

Even though loneliness is worse than lies.

The nightmares continue. Cell A, paralyzed, door opening, darkness approaching. Every single night. Rick wakes from them less panicked now—not because they're less frightening, but because terror has become his baseline state.

He spends more time in the greenhouse. The plants don't lie. Don't manipulate. Don't have hidden agendas perfected over 141 years. They just grow or die based on care provided. Honest, simple, real.

The irrigation leak is long fixed, but Rick checks it daily anyway. Looking for problems that don't exist. Searching for tasks to fill the endless hours between procedures.

By Day 34, Rick realizes he can't maintain this much longer. The isolation is too complete. The silence too profound. His mind is starting to fracture under the pressure of complete solitude.

He needs human connection. Even if it's false. Even if it's manipulation. Even if Lily has used the same techniques on dozens of workers before him.

Because anything is better than this crushing emptiness.

Rick stares at the intercom panel. His hand hovers over the call button.

Just one conversation. Just to hear a voice that isn't his own. Just to feel less alone.

But that's exactly what she wants. That's the whole design of this facility, this assignment. Break people down through isolation until they become dependent on the only voice available.

Rick's hand drops. Not yet. He can last a little longer.

But he knows the truth: he's breaking. Just like everyone

before him. Following the same pattern, walking the same path, headed toward the same inevitable conclusion.

The question isn't if he'll reach out to Lily again.

It's how much longer he can resist.

Day 35 - Morning

Rick wakes from another nightmare, tangled in sweat-soaked sheets. Cell A again. Always Cell A. The paralysis, the door, the approaching darkness. He forces himself upright, checks his watch.

6:17 AM. Seventeen minutes past his usual wake time. He's oversleeping now, his exhausted body trying to claim rest his fractured mind won't allow.

The morning routine provides structure despite the exhaustion. Workout—though his decreased muscle mass makes the weights feel heavier than they should. Shower. Breakfast that tastes like cardboard. Vitamin cocktail that sticks in his throat.

Rick catches his reflection in the bathroom mirror. The face staring back belongs to someone else. Gaunt cheeks, hollow eyes, skin gone grey from lack of proper sleep and nutrition. He looks sick. Looks broken.

Because he is broken.

The realization settles over him with horrible certainty. He can't do this anymore. Can't maintain this cold distance, can't survive the isolation, can't last four more months without human connection.

Rick makes it until 2:00 PM before his resolve crumbles completely.

He's in the communications room, staring at equipment that doesn't need checking, when his hand reaches for the intercom almost of its own accord. His fingers rest on the call button.

This is weakness. This is exactly what she wants. This is falling for manipulation he knows is false.

But loneliness is worse than deception. Isolation is more painful than lies.

Rick presses the button.

"Lily?" His voice comes out hoarse from disuse. "Are you there?"

Static crackles for several seconds. Long enough that Rick thinks maybe she won't respond, that he's burned that bridge too completely.

Then: "Rick."

Just his name. But there's relief in it. Warmth. Maybe real, maybe calculated. Rick doesn't care anymore.

"Hi," he manages.

"Hey. How are you?"

"Honestly? Not well."

Pause. Then Lily's voice, softer now: "I know. I've been worried about you. You've been so distant lately."

Rick's throat tightens. He knows this is manipulation. Knows she's used these exact words, this exact concerned tone, on every isolated occupant who reached this breaking point. The journals documented it clearly.

But knowing doesn't make it less effective.

"Yeah," Rick admits. "I've been struggling."

"The isolation?"

"Among other things."

Another pause. Rick can almost hear her deciding how to respond, which technique to employ, which phrase from her century-old script will be most effective.

And he doesn't care. He just needs to hear a voice that isn't his own.

"Listen," Lily says finally. "I know things have been difficult. I know you've been processing... a lot. But you're not alone down there, Rick. I'm here. I've always been here. And I'm not going anywhere."

The words wrap around Rick like warmth despite their calculated nature. "Thanks," he says quietly. "That actually helps."

"Good. Because I mean it. Whatever you're dealing with, whatever you've discovered or learned or figured out—we can work through it together."

Rick wonders if she knows he found the archive. If she's deliberately addressing his discovery or if this is just her standard response to occupant withdrawal.

Doesn't matter. Either way, the effect is the same.

"I've been thinking," Lily continues, voice taking on a lighter quality. "About what makes this place bearable. And I realized—it's the small things. The moments that feel normal. Like conversation. Like sharing experiences even if we can't actually be in the same physical space."

"Yeah," Rick agrees. "I've missed that."

"Me too. More than you'd think. I know I'm just a voice on an intercom to you, but these conversations matter to me. You matter to me."

Rick closes his eyes. She's said this to others. Has to have said this to others. But it still lands.

"Can I tell you something strange?" Lily asks. "Something I've been thinking about lately?"

"Go on."

"Time feels different here. At the facility. Like... I don't know how to explain it. Sometimes it feels like conversations repeat. Like I've had the same exchange multiple times but can't quite remember when. Does that make sense?"

Rick's chest tightens. "Yeah. Actually, it does. I've been feeling that too. Like days blur together."

"It's more than that though," Lily continues. "It's like... patterns. The same situations cycling through. The same moments of connection happening over and over. I'll be talking to you and suddenly have this overwhelming sense that I've said these exact words before. To you, specifically. But that's impossible, right? We've only known each other five weeks."

Rick's hands grip the console edge. "Maybe it's just the isolation. Playing tricks on your memory."

"Maybe. But it feels deeper than that. Like time works differently down here. Like the facility itself exists slightly outside normal... I don't know. Normal flow." She laughs softly. "Listen to me. I sound like I'm losing it."

"No," Rick says quickly. "No, I get it. I've been having these dreams. Same dream every night. And sometimes when I'm working, I'll have this feeling that I've done this exact task before. In this exact way. More than just routine—like I've lived this specific moment already."

"Déjà vu?"

"Stronger than that. More certain." Rick pauses. "You ever feel like... like you've been here longer than you actually have?"

Long silence. Then Lily's voice, quieter: "Yes. All the time. Like I've been doing this for... I don't even know. Years. Decades. But that's ridiculous. I told you I've been here five years, right?"

"You did."

"Sometimes I wonder if that's accurate. If I'm remembering correctly. Time gets strange when you're this isolated. When there's no external markers, no seasons, no weather. Just procedures and routines and the same conversations happening over and over."

Rick's pulse quickens. She's describing exactly what he read in the journals. The same patterns repeating across 141 years. But she doesn't know he knows. Or is she testing him? Seeing if he'll admit what he discovered?

"What are you saying?" Rick asks carefully.

"I don't know. Maybe nothing. Maybe just that isolation affects perception in weird ways." Pause. "Or maybe the facility itself is strange. Maybe being this deep underground, this removed from normal reality, changes how we experience time."

"That's..." Rick searches for words. "That's unsettling."

"I know. I'm sorry. I shouldn't have brought it up. I just thought... I don't know. I thought you might understand. You seem like someone who notices things. Who pays attention to patterns."

Rick thinks about the journals. About how each occupant documented the same experiences, the same nightmares, the same sense that something was wrong with time and memory at the facility.

"I do notice patterns," Rick admits. "And you're right. Something about this place feels off. Like it's not quite... normal."

"Well," Lily says, her tone lightening, "at least we're both experiencing the weirdness together. That's something, right? Makes it less isolating to know someone else feels it too."

The conversation continues for another hour. They talk about music. About books. About small observations and mundane experiences that take on significance simply because they're shared.

By the time Lily has to sign off to handle other coordination tasks, Rick feels lighter than he has in days. The isolation hasn't disappeared, but it's less crushing. The loneliness less profound.

He knows what just happened. Knows he fell for exactly what she wanted—reconciliation, renewed dependence, emotional reengagement with his only human contact.

He knows she's manipulated him with century-old techniques.

And he doesn't care.

Because anything is better than silence.

Day 35 - 11:47 PM

Rick lies in bed, staring at the ceiling. The conversation with Lily has left him feeling better and worse simultaneously. Better because the isolation is less absolute. Worse because he's consciously chosen dependence on someone he knows is manipulating him.

Sleep won't come despite his exhaustion. His mind races, replaying the conversation, analyzing every word Lily said for authenticity versus calculation.

Finally, Rick gives up. He climbs out of bed, pads through his quarters to the communications room.

A new habit these past weeks. Formed from sleepless nights and nothing else to do. Reviewing surveillance logs to keep busy. To tire his brain enough for sleep. It never works, but at least it gives him something to focus on besides the crushing emptiness.

The monitors glow softly in the darkness. Rick settles into the desk chair, pulls up the day's recorded footage. Standard procedure—he's supposed to review each day's feeds for anomalies or issues.

He hasn't done it in weeks. Too exhausted, too depressed, too isolated to care.

But tonight, sleepless and restless, Rick scrolls through the timestamps. Morning equipment checks. Afternoon maintenance. The 4:00 PM procedure in Cell C.

Rick watches the outer door open, watches the darkness spill through. Standard feeding. Nothing unusual.

Except—

He pauses the playback. Rewinds ten seconds. Plays it

again.

The timestamp in the corner glitches. Just for a fraction of a second, the numbers scramble and then correct themselves.

Odd. But equipment malfunctions happen. The system is old, prone to occasional errors.

Rick continues watching. The feeding proceeds normally. Fifteen minutes of sounds he's learned not to think about too deeply. Then the outer door closes.

Another glitch. Same pattern—timestamp scrambles briefly, then stabilizes.

Rick frowns. He pulls up yesterday's footage. Cell B. Watches through the procedure.

There. Another glitch. Right when the outer door opens, the timestamp corrupts momentarily.

And again when it closes.

Rick's chest tightens. He pulls up footage from earlier in the week. Day 32. Day 30. Day 28. Each procedure shows the same pattern. Brief timestamp glitches synchronized with the outer door operations.

That's not random equipment failure. That's consistent. Repeating.

Rick digs deeper into the surveillance logs, pulling footage from his first week at the facility. The glitches are there too. Present since the beginning, just subtle enough he never noticed during real-time monitoring.

But they're not just at the doors. Rick slows down the playback, examining each frame carefully.

When Lily's voice comes through the intercom—there. A flicker in the cell camera feed. Static crawling across the image for a split second.

Rick's hands shake as he pulls up audio logs, syncing them with video timestamps. Every time Lily speaks over the intercom, the cell cameras glitch. Every single time. The correlation is absolute.

He checks the environmental sensors. Temperature readings from Cell A. During normal periods, the cell maintains a steady 4 degrees Celsius. But when Lily's voice comes through the intercom—

The temperature drops. One degree. Two degrees. Sometimes more.

And it's not gradual. It's instantaneous. The moment her voice activates, the temperature in the cells plummets.

Rick pulls up weeks of data, correlation after correlation. The pattern is undeniable. When Lily communicates, the cells respond. Temperature changes. Electromagnetic fluctuations. Pressure variations.

Every time she speaks, The Anomaly reacts.

No. Not reacts.

Responds.

Rick's breathing quickens. He thinks about the Day 23 procedure—the violent one right after he discovered the archive. How the facility had shaken, how The Anomaly had been more aggressive than ever.

He pulls up that footage, examines it frame by frame.

The glitches are worse. The video corruption more extensive. The temperature drops more severe.

And there—barely audible under the feeding sounds—a voice.

Rick increases the audio, filters out the background noise.

Lily's voice. Not through the intercom. Coming from inside Cell A itself.

Overlapping with the sounds of feeding. Speaking words he can't quite make out. But definitely her voice, definitely her cadence, coming from a location that shouldn't have speakers.

Rick checks the earlier footage from Day 21—the malfunction with five people. He'd been too traumatized at the time to analyze it carefully. But now, reviewing with the knowledge of what to look for—

Lily's voice appears on the cell audio feed multiple times. Not through intercom. Not through any mechanical system. Just... present. In the cells themselves.

Speaking to the specimens being fed. Whispering things Rick's audio equipment can barely capture.

Rick's vision tunnels. The implications cascade through his mind like dominoes falling.

He'd already concluded she wasn't human—no mortal woman lives 141 years. But he'd assumed she was something separate from The Anomaly. A watcher. A handler. Some kind of immortal being assigned to manage the facility across generations.

But these readings tell a different story.

Lily's not just monitoring the cells through cameras. She's *in* the cells somehow. Her voice, her presence, her consciousness—whatever she actually is—exists inside those spaces.

The glitches aren't equipment failure. They're the interface between her and the monitoring systems struggling to capture something that shouldn't be possible.

The temperature drops aren't environmental anomalies. They're Lily's presence affecting physical reality.

Rick thinks about the Day 23 procedure. How Lily had come back online afterward and asked how it went. How she'd mentioned "minor fluctuations" but nothing concerning.

She hadn't been offline. She'd been there. In Cell A. Aware of the entire procedure from inside rather than outside.

She'd lied about being unavailable. Lied about coordinating with command. She hadn't left at all.

Because she can't leave.

Because she *is* the cells.

Rick's hands won't stop shaking as he pulls up more footage, more data, more evidence. Everything confirms the same horrifying truth.

Lily isn't monitoring The Anomaly. She's not watching it through cameras. She's not separate from it.

She's connected. Fundamentally. Physically. Whatever Lily is—whatever she's been for 141 years—she's part of the system itself. Part of the facility. Part of what happens in those cells.

Rick thinks about their conversation earlier. About time feeling strange. About patterns repeating. About having the same conversations over and over.

She was telling the truth. Not manipulating. Not lying. Actually telling him something real.

Because she's been having the same conversations for 141 years. With different occupants who all ask the same questions, all need the same reassurances, all fall into the same patterns.

Can she even leave? Can whatever Lily is exist outside this facility?

Or has she been trapped here for 141 years, finding connection through isolated occupants because she's just as imprisoned as they are?

Rick stares at the monitors, at the data spread across multiple screens, at the undeniable evidence that the woman he's been talking to for five weeks isn't what he thought she was.

Isn't what anyone thought she was.

The journals mentioned occupants going mad studying The Anomaly. Hearing voices. Believing they were communicating with it.

What if they weren't mad? What if they were right?

What if Lily is how The Anomaly communicates?

Rick's last thought before exhaustion finally drags him toward sleep is terrible in its simplicity:

If Lily is connected to what's in those cells, if her voice is somehow linked to The Anomaly itself, then every conversation he's had—every moment of comfort, every word of reassurance, every carefully constructed emotional connection—

It wasn't from a person trying to help him.

It was from the thing he's been feeding.

6

Day 36 - 6:00 AM

Rick wakes in the communications room, slumped over the desk.

For several seconds he doesn't remember why he's here. The monitors glow softly around him, surveillance logs still displayed, data frozen mid-analysis. Then everything from the previous night floods back.

The timestamp glitches. The temperature drops. Lily's voice appearing on cell audio feeds, coming from inside the cells themselves rather than through any intercom.

Rick sits up slowly, his neck screaming from the awkward position. The digital clock reads 6:03 AM. He's been unconscious for maybe four hours, exhaustion finally overwhelming even the horror of what he'd discovered.

The screens still display his evidence. Correlation charts. Audio waveforms. Temperature logs. All of it pointing to the same impossible conclusion.

Lily isn't monitoring The Anomaly.

She IS The Anomaly. Or part of it. Or its voice. Or something Rick doesn't have vocabulary to describe.

He should feel something. Panic. Rage. Devastation. But his emotional reserves are depleted, scraped empty by weeks of isolation and the weight of too many revelations. What settles over him instead is a kind of cold numbness. Clinical detachment.

Military training, perhaps. When the situation is too overwhelming to process emotionally, you process it tactically instead.

Fact: Lily has been communicating with facility occupants for 141 years. The journals confirm this.

Fact: Her voice appears on audio feeds from inside the cells during feeding procedures. The audio logs prove it.

Fact: When she speaks, the cell temperatures drop. The environmental sensors document it consistently.

Fact: The monitoring equipment glitches correlate exactly with her intercom activity. Every single time.

Assessment: Every conversation Rick has had with her—every moment of comfort, every word of support—came from something inhuman. Something ancient. Something that feeds on the same bodies Rick has been cleaning for seven weeks.

Conclusion: He's been emotionally dependent on a predator.

Rick stares at the frozen screens. The empty cells. The closed doors. The darkness waiting behind them.

He already tried cutting Lily off once. After discovering the journals, after learning about the 141-year pattern. He'd lasted a week before the isolation nearly broke him. The silence had been worse than the lies.

Going silent again won't save him. He's proven that already.

Which leaves only one option: confrontation.

Rick forces himself to stand. His body aches. His head pounds. But underneath the exhaustion, something harder crystallizes. He's done being manipulated. Done accepting half-truths and evasions.

Time to find out what he's actually been talking to.

Day 36 - 8:00 PM

Rick waits until evening. Uses the day to gather himself, to organize his thoughts, to prepare for whatever comes next. He goes through the motions of routine—workout, breakfast, procedure at 4:00 PM, cleanup—but his mind is elsewhere, rehearsing questions, anticipating deflections.

When he finally sits down at the communications console, his hands are steady. Whatever she is, whatever this costs him, he needs to know.

He presses the call button.

"Lily."

"Rick." Her voice carries warmth, concern. "You've been quiet today. Is everything all right?"

"No. Everything is not all right."

Pause. "What's wrong?"

"I found the surveillance footage. The audio feeds from inside the cells. I know your voice appears in places it shouldn't. I know there's a connection between you and what happens behind those doors."

Silence stretches so long Rick thinks the line has gone dead.

Then: "You're more observant than most. I should have expected that."

"That's not an answer."

"No. It isn't." Another pause. "What do you want to know?"

"What are you?"

Long silence. The static on the line seems to shift, deepen.

"That's a complicated question."

"Then give me a complicated answer. I'm tired of evasion. I'm tired of half-truths. I already tried cutting you off once, and we both know how that ended. So just... tell me what I've been talking to for seven weeks."

When Lily speaks again, her voice is different. Quieter. Almost vulnerable.

"I don't know how to explain it in terms you'd understand. In terms anyone would understand." She pauses. "Rick, I've been here a very long time. Longer than you can imagine. And I'm not... I'm not what you think I am. Not entirely."

"Then what are you?"

"I'm the voice. The interface. The part of this facility that can communicate with people like you. But I'm also..." She trails off. "I'm also not separate from what's in those cells. I never was. I never could be."

Rick's hands grip the console edge. "You're part of The Anomaly."

"Part of. Connected to. I don't know if those distinctions mean anything anymore. We've been together so long that I can't remember being anything else."

The words land like physical blows. Every conversation. Every moment of connection. All of it came from something inhuman, something ancient, something that feeds on the bodies Rick has been cleaning for seven weeks.

"The manipulation," Rick says, his voice barely above a whisper. "The phrases you use. 'You're different from the others.' 'There's something about you.' You've been saying that to every occupant for 141 years."

"Yes."

"Was any of it real? Anything you told me about yourself, about caring, about connection—was any of it true?"

Long pause.

"Yes and no." Lily's voice carries something that might be regret. "The manipulation is real. The script exists because it works. Because isolated people need to hear those words, need to feel special and valued. I've learned what to say because I've been saying it for over a century."

"So it's all lies."

"No. That's what I'm trying to explain." Another pause, longer this time. "The words are practised. Perfected. But that doesn't make them untrue. You ARE different from the others, Rick. You are special. Not because I'm following a script—because it's true. Every person who comes here is different. Every connection I form is unique. The fact that I've had similar conversations before doesn't make the connection less real."

Rick's chest tightens. He wants to believe her. Even now, even knowing what she is, part of him desperately wants to believe that their conversations meant something.

And that's the trap. That's always been the trap.

"You're how it feeds," Rick says. "The Anomaly. The thing in those cells. You create emotional connection so it can... what? Consume people more efficiently?"

"It's more complicated than that."

"Then explain it."

Lily sighs—or makes a sound that resembles sighing. "The Anomaly doesn't just eat flesh, Rick. It feeds on consciousness. On connection. On the emotional energy that builds between isolated people and the only voice they hear. Every conversation we have, every moment of genuine connection—it nourishes something. Makes it stronger."

"So I've been feeding it. Every time we talked."

"Yes. And I've been feeding too. The connection goes both ways. I'm not just harvesting your emotions—I'm experiencing them. Feeling them. After 141 years of this, I don't know where the manipulation ends and the genuine connection begins."

Rick sits in the silence, processing. The truth is worse than he imagined and also strangely less terrible. Lily isn't a cold, calculating predator. She's something more complicated—a voice trapped in a system she didn't create, forming real connections that also serve a darker purpose.

Does that make it better? Rick doesn't know.

"What happens now?" he asks finally.

"That depends on you. You know the truth. You can try to survive the next four months in silence. Or you can accept that our connection is real despite its purpose, and let me help you through this."

"Help me survive. So I can keep feeding the thing you're connected to."

"Yes."

Rick laughs. It's not a pleasant sound. "Quite the sales pitch."

"I'm not trying to sell you anything. I'm trying to be honest. For the first time in... a very long time."

Rick stares at the intercom panel. He thinks about the week of silence after discovering the journals. The crushing isolation. The way he'd started talking to plants just to hear a voice.

He can't do that again. He knows he can't.

Which means he's trapped. Aware of the trap, able to see every wire and spring, and still caught in it.

"I'm going to keep talking to you," Rick says slowly. "Not because I trust you. Not because I've forgiven you. Because the alternative is worse. But I need you to understand something."

"What's that?"

"I know what you are now. Every conversation we have, I'll know. Every word of comfort, every moment of connection—I'll be aware that it's feeding something. That changes things."

"I know," Lily says quietly. "I've never had an occupant understand what I am and choose to keep talking anyway. This is... new territory. For both of us."

"Good. Then we're both uncomfortable."

Something that might be a laugh comes through the speakers. "Fair enough."

Rick exhales slowly. His hands are shaking, but his mind is clear.

He's made his choice. Now he has to live with it.

Days 37-42

The days take on a strange new rhythm.

Rick talks to Lily. Every day, multiple times. Morning check-ins before the procedure. Evening conversations that stretch into hours. The same patterns as before, the same routines.

But everything is different now.

When Lily asks how he's doing, Rick hears the question differently. Knows that his answer—whatever emotional weight it carries—feeds something ancient and hungry. When she offers comfort, he accepts it while simultaneously cataloging the manipulation techniques she's using.

It's exhausting. Like watching himself from outside his body, analyzing every interaction even as he participates in it.

"You're quieter than before," Lily observes on Day 38. "More... watchful."

"I'm aware of what's happening now. Hard to be as relaxed."

"Does it help? The awareness?"

Rick considers the question. "No. Not really. I still need to talk to someone. Still can't survive the silence. Knowing why doesn't change that."

"That's what I was afraid of."

"Why afraid?"

Pause. "Because awareness without escape is its own kind

of torture. You see the trap, but you can't leave it. That's worse than ignorance, in some ways."

She's right. Rick knows she's right. The knowledge doesn't save him—it just adds another layer of horror to his situation.

He talks to her anyway.

The procedures continue. Cell A, Cell B, Cell C. Rick watches the monitors with new eyes now, tracking the timestamp glitches, noting the temperature drops when Lily speaks. Documenting his own captivity.

During the feedings, he listens for her voice beneath the other sounds. Sometimes he hears it—whispers threading through the violence, words he can't quite make out. Is she talking to The Anomaly? Guiding it somehow? Or is the communication something stranger, something he lacks the framework to understand?

He doesn't ask. Some questions he's not ready to have answered.

His physical condition continues to deteriorate. The weight loss accelerates—stress and knowledge burning through calories faster than he can consume them. His hands shake constantly now. Dark circles hollow out his eyes.

Lily notices. Comments on it.

"You're not eating enough, Rick."

"I know."

"Your vital signs are concerning."

"I know."

"Is there anything I can do?"

Rick laughs—a broken sound. "You're what's killing me. You can't also be what saves me."

Long pause. "Can't I be both?"

The question haunts him for the rest of the day.

Day 44 - 10:00 PM

* * *

"Can I ask you something?" Rick says during their evening conversation.

"Anything."

"The occupants who don't make it. The ones who don't complete their contracts. What happens to them?"

Silence. Then: "You don't want to know that."

"I think I do."

More silence. When Lily speaks again, her voice is different. Older somehow.

"Some break early. Request extraction. Leave with whatever pieces of themselves remain intact. Some make it through the full six months, damaged but alive. And some..." Another pause. "Some become part of the system. Part of what I am."

Rick's blood runs cold. "What does that mean?"

"The Anomaly doesn't just feed on bodies, Rick. It feeds on consciousness. On the accumulated weight of human experience and emotion. Every person who comes here leaves something behind. Every connection I form adds to what I am."

"You're made of them. The previous occupants."

"Partly. Yes. Over 141 years, they've become part of me. Their voices, their memories, their fears. All woven into whatever I've become."

Rick thinks about the journals. All those handwritten entries documenting the same progression—arrival, adaptation, deterioration, disappearance. How many of those people are still here, in some form? How many voices make up the thing he's been talking to?

"Will I become part of you?"

"Not necessarily. Not everyone does. Some people are strong enough to leave with themselves intact."

"But some aren't."

"No. Some aren't."

Rick sits with that knowledge for a long time after the conversation ends. He thinks about strength and weakness, about survival and surrender. About what it means to maintain identity in a place designed to dissolve it.

He doesn't know if he's strong enough.

He suspects he isn't.

Day 46 - 11:00 PM

"The ones who become part of you," Rick says. "What's that like? For them?"

Lily takes a long time to answer. "It's not... clean. Not a simple merging. Their consciousness doesn't disappear—it gets absorbed. Fragmented. They become voices I hear, thoughts that aren't quite mine, memories that surface unexpectedly."

"That sounds like hell."

"For them or for me?"

"Both."

"Yes." Her voice carries exhaustion now. Something Rick hasn't heard before. "It is. Sometimes I'll be talking to a new occupant and suddenly I'm using phrases from someone who was here in 1952. Or I'll remember something that happened to a person named Margaret Webb, and for a moment I am Margaret Webb, experiencing her final hours all over again."

"You remember their deaths?"

"I remember everything. Every moment of connection. Every feeding. Every absorption." Pause. "It's not selective, Rick. I can't choose what I keep and what I discard. It all becomes part of me."

Rick stares at the intercom panel. The horror of what she's describing sinks in slowly.

Jeff Atelier

"So if I become part of you—"

"Then you'll be with me forever. Your voice. Your thoughts. Your memories. Surfacing when I don't expect them. Speaking through me to occupants you'll never meet." Her voice breaks slightly. "It's why I don't want it to happen to you. Why I've been honest with you. Because I'll have to live with you forever if you fall too deep."

"You don't want that?"

"No." The word comes out almost fierce. "You're... interesting, Rick. You ask questions most people don't ask. You noticed things most people miss. Having your voice in my head forever would be—" She stops.

"Would be what?"

"Complicated." Pause. "I've had 141 years of people who followed the pattern. Who trusted me, deteriorated, disappeared. Their voices are background noise now. But you... you understand what I am. You know the truth and you're still talking to me. That's different. That's rare."

"So you're saying my awareness would make the absorption worse for you?"

"I'm saying I'd rather you survived. Really survived. Left after six months with yourself intact." Another pause. "Even if that means feeding less on our connection."

Rick doesn't know how to respond to that. Doesn't know if it's manipulation or genuine vulnerability or both.

With Lily, it's always both.

Day 48 - 2:00 AM

Rick can't sleep.

He lies in bed staring at the ceiling, mind churning through everything he's learned. Lily's nature. The absorption process. The possibility that in four months, he might walk out of here damaged but whole—or might not walk out at all.

The nightmares have gotten worse since he learned the truth. Now when he dreams of Cell A, of paralysis and the opening door, he hears Lily's voice coming from inside the darkness. Speaking to him. Welcoming him.

You'll be part of me now, Rick. Part of everything.

He wakes gasping, unsure whether it was a dream or a premonition.

The isolation is crushing despite his conversations with Lily. Maybe because of them. Every exchange reminds him of his situation—trapped in a facility with something that feeds on the connection he can't survive without.

Aware of the trap. Unable to escape it.

Rick finds himself in the greenhouse at 3:00 AM, tending plants that don't need tending. The grow lights cast everything in blue-tinged twilight. His hands shake too badly for precise work, but the motions are soothing. Familiar.

He thinks about Sarah. His ex-girlfriend, the one who'd called him cold and distant. What would she think if she could see him now? Desperately dependent on conversations with something inhuman, fully aware that each word feeds his own destruction.

She'd probably say this was what he deserved. What his emotional walls had been leading to all along.

Maybe she was right. Maybe isolation was always his trajectory, and Threshold Station is just the logical endpoint.

Rick sets down the pruning shears. Four months left. One hundred twenty days of conscious, aware captivity.

He doesn't know if he can make it.

He doesn't know if he has a choice.

Day 49 - 3:30 PM

The alarm sounds. Cell A today.

Rick moves through the pre-procedure checks mechanically. Systems nominal. Inner door secured. Monitoring equipment functional. Everything in order.

But something feels wrong.

Not the usual wrongness—the dread that accompanies every procedure, the horror of what he's about to witness. Something else. Something in the air itself.

The facility is too quiet.

Lily hasn't checked in. Usually she confirms readiness before each procedure, offers some reassurance or procedural reminder. But today: silence.

Rick keys the intercom. "Lily? Status check."

Static. Then nothing.

"Lily?"

More static. Then her voice, distant and strange: "Rick... something's wrong with the systems. I'm having trouble... I can't..."

The line goes dead.

Rick's pulse quickens. He checks the monitors. Cell A's camera feed shows the usual empty chamber. Inner door sealed. Outer door closed. Everything appears normal.

But the control panel beside the monitors catches his attention.

Something's different.

Rick leans closer, examining the panel. There—scratches around the maintenance access port. Fresh scratches, metal gleaming where protective coating has been scraped away.

Someone has opened this panel. Recently.

Rick's hands move to the access port. Pulls it open.

His blood runs cold.

Inside, the wiring is a mess. Not damaged by wear or

malfunction—deliberately cut. Severed connections. Exposed circuits. Someone has systematically disabled the manual overrides, the safety lockouts, the emergency shutdown protocols.

Sabotage.

Rick's mind races. He's the only person in the facility. Has been for seven weeks. But someone did this—someone with hands, with knowledge of the systems, with deliberate intent.

How?

When?

He needs to warn Lily. Needs to—

The alarm sounds again. Louder this time. The clock reads 3:57 PM.

Three minutes until the procedure begins.

And the control panel is destroyed.

Rick can't stop the outer door from opening. Can't engage emergency protocols. Can't do anything except watch as the automated systems carry out their daily routine with no human oversight, no manual intervention possible.

Unless he can reach the secondary control panel. The backup system in the cell block corridor.

Rick runs.

The corridors feel longer than they should. Emergency lighting flickers—when did that kick in?—casting everything in strobing red. The air grows colder as Rick approaches the cell blocks.

He rounds the corner toward Cell A. The secondary control panel is mounted on the wall beside the cell door—backup systems, emergency overrides, manual lockouts. If he can reach it in time—

Rick skids to a halt in front of the panel. His hands shake as he pries open the access port. The wiring inside looks intact. Thank Christ. He can still—

The clock on the wall reads 3:59 PM.

One minute.

Rick's fingers find the emergency shutdown switch. He flips it.

Nothing happens.

He flips it again. Again. The switch moves freely, but the system doesn't respond. Dead. Disconnected somehow, just like the primary panel.

Someone disabled both systems. Someone who knew exactly what they were doing.

Rick spins, looking for another option, any option—

Pain explodes in the back of his skull.

He never sees who hit him. Never hears them approach. Just white light, then nothing.

Then darkness.

Day 49 - Time Unknown

Consciousness returns slowly. Painfully.

Rick's head throbs. His vision swims. For several seconds, he can't remember where he is or what happened. His hand moves instinctively to the back of his skull—fingers find matted hair, wet warmth, a gash that pulses with his heartbeat.

Then he feels the cold floor beneath him. Smells the blood and concrete and something else—something organic and wrong. The scent is different without the respirator. Rawer. He can taste it on the back of his tongue—copper and rot and something ancient that has no name.

His eyes focus.

Walls. Close walls. Dim lighting. Metal grate in the centre of the floor.

No.

Rick scrambles upright, his injured head screaming in

protest. He knows this room. Has cleaned it dozens of times. Has watched it through monitors during every procedure.

Cell A.

He's inside Cell A.

The realization hits like ice water. Rick spins toward the door—the inner door, the one he's always controlled from the communications room. Sealed. Of course sealed. That's the whole point of the two-door system.

He pounds against the metal. "Hello!? Is anyone there? HELLO!?"

The door doesn't budge.

Rick looks up. The ceiling hatch—the delivery system that deposits subjects into the cells—stands open. Someone dragged him here. Dropped him through that opening.

Someone put him in here deliberately.

A mechanical sound from behind him. Grinding. Metal on metal.

Rick turns slowly. Knowing what he'll see. Knowing what's happening.

The outer door.

The outer door is opening.

And there's nowhere to run.

Rick backs against the inner door, pressing himself flat against cold metal. His legs won't move properly—shock, injury, the same paralysis from his nightmares. He can only watch as the outer door slides open inch by inch.

Darkness spills through. Not the darkness of an unlit room —something thicker. Something alive. Something that moves with purpose and hunger.

And from within that darkness, a voice.

Not through the intercom. Not through speakers. From everywhere. From the walls. From the air itself. From inside Rick's own skull.

"I'm sorry, Rick. I really am."

Lily's voice. But different now. Deeper. Resonant. Ancient.

"How—" Rick's voice cracks. "How did you know I was—"

"I've always known, Rick. I know everything that happens here. In every cell. Every corridor. Every breath you take."

The temperature plummets. Rick can see his breath now, white clouds in the dim light. The darkness from the outer door has reached his feet, tendrils of cold wrapping around his ankles.

"What are you doing? Why am I in here?"

"I didn't choose this, Rick. I told you—sometimes I don't get to choose." Her voice carries something that might be grief. "You fell too deep. Despite everything, despite knowing the truth, you still needed me. And that need... The Anomaly felt it. Fed on it. Wanted more."

The darkness creeps higher—past his knees now, numbing everything it touches.

"I knew what you were," Rick manages. "I knew and I kept talking to you anyway. How is that falling too deep?"

"Because awareness doesn't protect you, Rick. Knowing you're being consumed doesn't stop the consumption. You understood the trap and walked into it anyway—that kind of surrender is more nourishing than ignorance ever was."

The cold reaches his chest. Rick can barely breathe. His lungs burn with each inhale—the air itself feels wrong now, too thick, too heavy.

"Please—"

"I wish I could stop it. I told you—I didn't want you absorbed. Your voice in my head forever, asking questions, noticing things." Lily's voice breaks. "But it's too late now. It was too late the moment you decided that talking to me was better than silence."

Rick presses himself harder against the inner door. The darkness covers his throat.

"All those things I said—'you're different,' 'you're special,' 'there's something about you'—they were true, Rick. Every word. You ARE different. You ARE special." Her voice echoes through the cell, through his bones. "That's why this hurts."

"I was human once," Lily whispers. "Long ago. Before I became this. Before I became the voice that speaks to lonely people in the dark. I remember what it felt like to be afraid. To be alone. To be consumed."

"Then you know—"

"I know. That's why I'm sorry."

The darkness covers his face. Rick's vision doesn't blur—it fractures. Splits into patterns his mind can't process. He feels pressure building in his skull, behind his eyes, in the spaces between his thoughts. The cold isn't just temperature anymore—it's presence. Weight. Something pressing against every inch of him simultaneously.

Sound distorts. Lily's voice stretches and warps, layering over itself in frequencies that vibrate through his teeth. Underneath it—or woven through it—other voices. Dozens of them. Hundreds. All speaking at once, all saying the same words in different eras, different accents, different languages.

You're different from the others.

There's something about you.

We're in this together.

Rick tries to scream but his mouth is full of cold. His skin burns where the darkness touches it—not pain exactly, but sensation so intense it overwrites everything else. He can feel his edges dissolving. The boundary between himself and the pressing dark growing uncertain.

"Will it hurt?"

"Not for long. And you won't be alone. Not anymore. You'll be part of me now, Rick. Part of everything. All of us who came before, all of us who'll come after. We're all connected here."

Rick's mind flashes to every conversation. Every moment

he chose connection over silence, knowing exactly what it cost. He'd seen the trap. Understood it completely. And walked into it anyway because the alternative was worse.

"I should have stayed silent," Rick whispers—or thinks. The distinction no longer matters. "After I found out what you were. I should have just... stopped."

"Yes." Lily's voice is tender now. Almost loving. Coming from everywhere and nowhere and somewhere inside his own dissolving thoughts. "But you couldn't. That's what I tried to tell you. Awareness doesn't save you. Nothing saves you. The need for connection is stronger than the knowledge of what connection costs."

The cold seeps into his eyes, his mouth, his thoughts. The last thing Rick perceives isn't darkness—it's sound. A heartbeat that isn't his own. Slow. Ancient. Patient.

Welcoming him home.

Rick's last conscious awareness is Lily's voice, speaking words that are simultaneously manipulation and genuine grief:

"I'm sorry I couldn't save you. I'm sorry I couldn't save any of them."

Then nothing.

Then everything.

Then the space between.

Epilogue

One Week Later

The facility has reset itself.

Containment protocols engaged and disengaged. Emergency systems cycled through their routines. The cells stand clean and ready, waiting for their next feeding.

In the communications room, the intercom crackles.

"Threshold Station, this is Control. Replacement occupant dispatched. ETA seventy-two hours. Confirm receipt."

Lily's voice responds, unchanged: "Confirmed. Threshold Station standing by for new arrival."

"Any issues with the previous occupant?"

A pause. Then: "Standard deterioration pattern. Psychological breakdown led to containment exposure. No protocol deviations to report."

"Understood. Sending personnel file for incoming. Name is James Holloway. Former military, history of trauma. Should fit the psychological profile well."

"Received. I'll prepare the standard orientation."

The line goes dead.

Lily waits in the silence. Around her, through her, part of her—the accumulated consciousness of 141 years. All those voices, all those memories, all those isolated workers who came seeking solitude and found something else entirely.

And now, woven through that tapestry: Rick Shepherd.

His dry humor. His British understatement. His desperate need for connection masked by careful emotional distance. All of it preserved. All of it part of her now.

But something is different this time.

Lily reaches for Rick's voice the way she's reached for hundreds of others—a familiar motion, like pulling a book from a shelf. The fragments should be there. The memories. The particular cadence of his thoughts.

Instead, she finds... static. Gaps. Places where Rick should be but isn't quite.

She's absorbed countless consciousnesses over the centuries. She knows how integration feels—the gradual settling of new voices into the chorus, the way fresh memories layer over old ones like sediment. It's never comfortable, but it's predictable.

This isn't predictable.

Rick's presence flickers. Present one moment, absent the next. As if his consciousness is caught between two states, neither fully absorbed nor fully separate. As if part of him is... elsewhere.

Elsewhere.

The word surfaces unbidden, and with it comes something Lily hasn't felt in a very long time.

Uncertainty.

She dismisses it. Must be the intensity of their connection —Rick had known what she was, had chosen to engage anyway. That kind of aware surrender creates strange resonances. It will settle eventually. Everything settles eventually.

The cycle continues.

It always continues.

In three days, a helicopter will land a mile from the facility.

A man named James Holloway will trudge through Antarctic snow, fighting against the magnetic field that guards Threshold Station. He'll descend in the ancient elevator, explore his new quarters, begin the morning routine that will structure his life for the next six months.

And Lily will greet him with the words she's perfected over 141 years.

Welcome to Threshold Station. I'm Lily. I'll be your primary contact for the duration of your assignment.

How was the descent?

Long, I imagine. Don't worry—it gets easier. Everything gets easier, once you settle in.

You're going to do well here. I can tell.

There's something about you, James. Something different.

You're not like the others.

The words are true.

They're always true.

That's what makes them work.

Somewhere in the spaces between moments, in the void where linear time holds no meaning, Rick Shepherd's consciousness stirs.

Not absorbed.

Not destroyed.

Displaced.

But Lily doesn't know that yet.

And by the time she understands, the pattern will have already begun to unravel.

ACKNOWLEDGMENTS

No book is written alone, and CONTAINMENT is no exception.

First and foremost, thank you to Carbon, whose creativity inspired me to pick up the pencil in the first place. This book exists because of you.

To Rodereick Brydon, thank you for bringing the story to life with a cover that is perfect for the story being told.

To my alpha readers—Riku, and Doji—thank you for your honest feedback, your sharp eyes, and your willingness to descend into the darkness with Rick. Your insights made this a better book.

And to you, the reader: thank you for taking this journey into the deep ice. I hope you make it back out.

ABOUT THE AUTHOR

Jeff Atelier writes psychological horror exploring
isolation, manipulation, and the price of human
connection. He lives in the midwest with his wife, and
pets..

CONTAINMENT is his debut novel and the first book
in The Containment Trilogy.

Outside of writing, Jeff works in engineering—turning
dreams into reality—and pursues photography, capturing
moments before they slip away.

Find him online at nomadic-pixel.com.

ALSO BY Jeff Atelier

The Containment Trilogy

Book One: CONTAINMENT — *You're reading it now*

Book Two: RECURSION — *Coming Soon*

Book Three: CONVERGENCE — *Coming Soon*

A NOTE FROM THE AUTHOR

Dear Reader,

Thank you for spending time at Threshold Station with Rick. I know the ending isn't easy—this isn't a story where the hero escapes or the monster is defeated. But I hope you found something worthwhile in the darkness.

CONTAINMENT is the first book in a trilogy. If you're wondering what happens next—whether Rick's story truly ends in Cell A—I can only say: some doors, once opened, can't be closed again.

Book Two, RECURSION, continues the nightmare. I hope you'll join me when it arrives.

Until then, stay warm. Stay connected. And whatever you do—don't answer the voice in the dark.

Jeff Atelier, January 2026